Longing for the Moon
(Tales of Magic, Mystery, Wonder, and Sorrow)

David P. Fallon

a DSTL arts publication

Longing for the Moon

a DSTL Arts publication

The work in this book was written by David P. Fallon, a participant in DSTL Arts's Arts Mentorship Program, and first printed in September, 2019 by DSTL Arts publishing in Los Angeles, CA, U.S.A. All rights reserved. No part of this book may be reproduced in any form without written permission from the publisher.

Cover Design: Luis Antonio Pichardo

Original Cover Image/Art: Susan Chavez
(follow on Instagram using @chicanasusie)

Book Design: Luis Antonio Pichardo

ISBN: 978-1-946081-32-2

10 9 8 7 6 5 4 3 2 1

www.DSTLArts.org

Los Angeles, CA

For my Mother

Table of Contents

Pablo 1

Christmas After 6

The Fish's Wishes 8

The Meaning of Grief 10

The Writer 13

Stuart 15

10 22

The Rainbow 25

Longing for the Moon 27

The Walk 29

Pecker 33

Man and the Devil 36

The Social Worker 38

RV 42

A Boy and His Dog 44

The Albatross 47

The Man on the Moon 52

The Wind 55

Chicken Suit Larry 56

Buddy & Dean	59
The Story of a Rock	62
Whiskers	65
The Old Coyote	67
For the Birds	69
The Ant	70
Green	73
Animal Courage	75
Death's Dilemma	81
The Backyard War	83
Living In a Truck	88
Life at the Lake	90
Freedom of Imagination	93
Hilde	101
The Christmas Spam	106
Martin Luthers	108
The Egg	123

"We do not take moonlight for granted. It is like snow, or like dew on a July morning. It does not reveal but changes what it covers. And its low intensity—so much lower than daylight—makes us conscious that it is something added to the down, to give it, for only a little time, a singular and marvelous quality that we should admire while we can, for soon it will be gone again."

– **Richard Adams;** *Watership Down*

Pablo

Mike found a penguin on the beach. It wasn't moving, and it looked like it might be sick.

"Don't touch it," a passerby insisted. "It might have a disease."

All the more reason for me to see if I can help it, thought Mike. So he gently lifted the penguin into a small sack and carried it home. The penguin did not resist.

Mike gave the penguin a shower with the hose to wash off the sand. He watched it shake the water from its feathers. He pulled open a can of sardines and offered one to the penguin, but the penguin turned away.

"Maybe you need some rest," Mike said. He put an old pillow in a box and cut a hole in the front. He carefully placed the penguin inside.

"I'll call you Pablo," Mike said to the penguin as he turned out the light and got into his own bed.

• • •

The next day before dawn, Mike was awakened by a loud, rolling, honking sound. He hopped out of bed with his heart pounding. The penguin was standing nearby staring up at him.

"You want something to eat?" Mike said, to which Pablo responded with a light growling noise.

Mike walked to the fridge and got out the can of sardines. Pablo quickly gobbled down every bite, after which he fluffed his feathers as if in delight.

"You like that, eh," Mike said as he served himself a breakfast of black toast and runny eggs.

After cleaning up, Mike grabbed his watering can and opened the door to head for the garden. Pablo shuffled after him, and as Mike did his chores around the yard, Pablo stayed with him.

Around lunchtime, Mike turned on the hose to give Pablo a shower. "You've earned it buddy," Mike said as Pablo happily fluffed his feathers.

As the days went by, Mike and Pablo became closer and closer. Mike would talk to Pablo as they worked together in the garden. It was the most talking he had done for a long time. Pablo seemed to like the sound of his voice and would sometimes add his distinct penguin sounds to the conversation.

Mike was sitting on the ground after pulling some weeds and discussing dinner options when suddenly Pablo stepped into his lap and nestled in close. At first Mike was taken aback. He didn't know what to do.

"Pablo was my best friend," Mike said with a faraway look. "We did everything together. And when everybody else started dying, like us old people do, for a long time it was just me and Pablo." Mike paused and sniffed loudly. Pablo the penguin looked up at him and made a gentle trilling sound.

"Pablo was good people," Mike said. "Just like you."

• • •

Several weeks went by this way with the two eating and spending the days together in the garden. Pablo was getting stronger every day and even began to help out by snatching beetles and slugs away from the flowers.

Then, after Mike had a Reuben sandwich for lunch and Pablo gulped down two dozen peeled shrimp, he looked at Pablo and said, "It's time to take a walk to the beach."

As the duo trundled down the street, people could not help but stop and stare. Mike simply nodded as he and Pablo passed. Pablo waddled on, obviously. Suddenly Mike's friend Benny appeared.

"What da hell is that?" he nearly screamed.

"This is Pablo," Mike said without looking at Benny.

"Well, pleased to meetcha, Pablo," Benny laughed as he reached toward the penguin. Pablo reared up, snatched Benny's fingers in his beak, and shook them violently.

"Damn! That crazy bird's got rabies!" Benny shouted as he lept back.

"Nah," Mike chuckled, "he's just shy of strangers."

Benny responded by marching off in an angry huff.

"You're a good judge of character," Mike winked. "Benny only comes around when he wants something."

When they finally reached the ocean, Mike stood for a long time watching the waves flow in and out. Pablo sat next to him preening his feathers with flicks of his beak. Each flick made his feathers shine more brightly. This was the moment Mike had been dreading. He was used to having Pablo around, even enjoyed his company. It had been so long since he had had decent company.

"You can go now if you want to," Mike said sadly.

Pablo looked up at Mike and made a few soft squeaks. He ambled slowly toward the water. When he reached the edge of the surf, he cocked his head toward Mike as if he were inviting him to come along.

"You take care of yourself," Mike called. And with a leap, Pablo disappeared beneath the waves.

Mike went home to a lonely dinner of spaghetti and meat sauce. He stowed the leftovers and cleaned the dishes before brushing his teeth. He nearly tripped over Pablo's box before getting into bed. Not yet wanting to let go of his friend, he stowed the box under his bed. His sleep was fitful, and when he did sleep, he dreamed he was in the ocean swimming side by side with Pablo.

• • •

A few months later, Mike got up to start his day. It had become habit to survey Pablo's box just in case the penguin had returned in the night. Unfortunately, Mike was disappointed again. He grabbed his watering can and went to the garden to pull some weeds. After a few hours, Mike was thinking about what to make for lunch when he heard Benny's voice in the distance.

"Hey, buddy!" Benny grinned as he pranced through the gate. "Got a favor to ask ya."

Mike cringed at those familiar, unwelcome words. He stood to greet his so-called friend with a reluctant handshake.

"I just need a hundred bucks," Benny nodded. "To pay some bills and stuff. You know I'm good for it." But of course Mike knew Benny was not good for it.

Mike was reaching for his wallet with a frown when there was a popping, boom-like low note from an angry trumpet. The sound made Benny jump as a small, black silhouette bolted through the open gate with wings outstretched.

"Get that thing away from me!" Benny squealed as he ran toward the street. "I told you it had rabies!"

"Great to see you," Mike said as Pablo rubbed his leg gently. He reached down to stroke Pablo's feathers, and Pablo made a rumbling purr in his throat.

"I have some filet of sole in the fridge," Mike said. "One of your favorites." And as the duo made their way toward the kitchen, Mike had an uncharacteristic smile on his face.

Christmas After

When Randy was seven years old, he thought the worst day of the year had to be January 2nd, which was the day most people dumped their Christmas trees on the side of the road. By the end of the week, sad piles of dried up trees were everywhere, waiting to be taken wherever old Christmas trees were taken. For a sensitive seven-year-old, the carnage was almost too much to bear.

When he was nine, Randy decided something had to be done about this annual holiday travesty. But being only nine, he had no idea what that something could be.

By his eleventh Christmas, Randy stopped believing in Santa Claus after waking up in the middle of the night and catching his mother hurriedly carrying beautifully wrapped gifts from the car to the living room. Months before, he harbored doubts about the jolly old fat man story as it seemed too bizarre to be true. Seeing his mother was the final proof. With the loss of Santa, his distaste for the annual Christmas tree dump was pretty much forgotten.

Until Randy had a child of his own.

Billy meant the world to Randy. He was Randy's reason for living, and indisputably the best thing that ever happened to him. Like most parents, Randy would do anything for him, so when Randy saw distressed five-year-old Billy noticing the piles of abandoned Christmas trees on January 2nd, his heart quickly sank straight back to his own childhood, and he knew had to do something about those damn trees.

Later that night, Randy borrowed his buddy's truck. He tossed in the back as many trees as it could hold and drove until he reached the nearby foothills. He found a clearing where he set up the abandoned trees to create a small forest. There were ten of them. Some were still draped with bedraggled strands of gold and silver tinsel. Randy brought out some old ornaments and quickly decorated his trees.

The next day, when Randy took his son to visit the trees, Billy's eyes and mouth gaped in wonder. He giggled and danced through the Christmas tree forest.

"Christmas after!" squealed Billy joyfully.

"You mean, after Christmas," Randy corrected.

"No," Billy disagreed. "Christmas After!"

Randy shrugged and smiled. It was as good a name as any.

The Fish's Wishes

A hungry little fish was about to gobble up a tiny snail when the snail shouted: "Wait! If you do not eat me, I will grant you three wishes!"

The fish agreed thinking that if the snail was lying he would just eat him. And even if the snail did grant the wishes, the fish would still eat him.

"Choose wisely," the snail warned. "For wishes have consequences."

First, the fish wished to be human. But the novelty of walking on land wore off quickly as the fish could not get use to the feel of the air on his dry skin or the boorish way the other humans talked.

Next, the fish wished to be a bird. He enjoyed immensely soaring through the skies and decided he would seek out the snail for a nice meal as he now had no more need for wishes. Before he could do so, a tremendous boom filled the sky. An unseen force knocked him to the ground. He plummeted to the ground where he lay dying from a gaping gunshot wound.

"I want to be back in the sea!" he called out his final wish.

The fish awoke in the water. He was still alive! He was so relieved. Until all of sudden a humongous, slimy thing oozed above him. Before he could react, the thing opened its tremendous maw and swallowed him whole.

"What happened??" he asked the darkness.

"When you wished to be back in the sea, you did not say what you wanted to be," said the voice of the snail. "So I turned you into a bit of algae, because I was hungry too."

And the last sound the fish heard before he was digested in the stomach of the snail was a loud, obnoxious burp.

The Meaning of Grief

Grief woke up depressed one day because she could not understand what her meaning was. She was sick and tired of being known as the worst emotion.

Dislike rolled his eyes and told everyone Grief was having a mid-life crisis.

Worry bought her several self-help books and showed her an online forum for persons suffering from personality problems.

Rage yelled at her in an AA, scared-straight sort of way which only made Grief feel worse.

Terror started to feel depressed too, and ran away screaming. An ambulance had to be called.

Silly could not stop laughing and kept drawing funny pictures of animals to try to cheer her up. Grief threw the pictures away.

Despair wept for her to the point where everyone just wanted him to go away.

Flirtatious kept trying to get her attention by brushing against her, but unfortunately he was one of the emotions Grief liked least of all.

Shy thought he might have some good advice as he was often depressed too, but he just couldn't get himself to talk to Grief.

Gullible hung out with Grief for a little while until he started to feel depressed himself.

Bored found the whole thing tedious and told Grief to just get over it.

Jealous spouted a monologue about the dozens of reasons she was envious of Grief. Grief thought it was the most ridiculous thing she ever heard.

Lazy overslept and missed his meeting with Grief. He tried to reschedule but by that time Grief stopped returning his phone calls and texts.

Overwhelmed had a panic attack when he remembered that he had been depressed in the past, and started obsessing that he would get that way again.

Mischievous thought it would cheer Grief up if he played a joke on her. It backfired and Grief nearly slapped his face.

Brave was fortunately able to step in and break up the fight.

Excited got jumpy and hopped around trying to tell Grief about the importance of her as an emotion to protect from harmful influences. This only left Grief more confused.

Annoyed, who could not stand Excited, got tangled up in the conversation, which turned into a noisy quarrel.

Sadness and Happiness tried to intervene together with their own theory about the importance of Grief. Their attempt became so convoluted by their contrariness that even Focused was unable to decipher their meaning.

Hate got too philosophical and religious, which completely turned Grief off.

Inspired was too poetic.

Enchanted, too lofty.

Strange, too obscure.

Intimidated, too shaky.

Intimidating, too mean.

Compassionate, too smarmy.

Spiteful, Destructive, Talkative, Guilty, Lonely, and so many other were just ripe pains in the ass as far as Grief was concerned.

Then came Love.

Love reached out and touched Grief in a way that no one else could. Grief suddenly started to cry, and she felt like all the thoughts and feelings were happening at the same time inside her. Every single one.

"And that, dear Grief, is your true power," Love said sweetly.

The Writer

"Write fearlessly," the old man told her shortly before he died. They were his last words.

"Do you know who that was?" the charge nurse asked Madison. Madison shrugged her shoulders and shook her head.

"Gallo Turnbill," her boss looked at Madison disapprovingly. "He wrote *Feathers Fly*. Only the best book ever written."

And 32 other books, Madison read on Wikipedia. These included mostly novels, a few collections of short stories, two memoirs, and a short series of spy novels one critic called: "better than Bond."

Madison was a NOC nurse at a state-run nursing facility. Gallo Turnbill spent his last days under her care before succumbing to cirrhosis of the liver at the age of 73.

After she found out who he was, Madison became a little obsessed. She read everything she could find about him. Most of his books had been written when he was in his 40s and 50s, before he divorced his wife of 25 years—a beautiful actress named Stella May. She eventually left him for a much younger, more handsome leading man. Following this heartbreak, Gallo Turnbill frittered away his money on gambling and booze. Besides the occasional article with the New Yorker, he never wrote significantly again.

Madison read all of his books beginning with *When January Comes*, which was a somewhat dismal affair with lines like: "The cold creeps in like a wall of iron that grips the life from his already lifeless soul".

Then there was *My Years in Tampa*, a much brighter work: "The sun shone on the bronze sand as the citrus tang of his lime margarita burned his mind eye". This one struck Madison as a hint of alcoholism to come.

Her favorite was *Bones of Britain* because it contained 62 pages of exploration on England's role in bringing the United States into World War II. Like her father, Madison had always been something of a WWII buff.

She hated *Feathers Fly*, her boss's personal favorite. It was Gallo Turnbill's poor attempt at a comedic novel. His sensibilities as a writer simply did not translate well into the realm of humor. As if in conformation of Madison's opinion, it was the only comedic novel he ever wrote.

Madison opened a box containing her old journals one night. She leafed through several volumes and lingered over passages that had been long forgotten, especially ones about wanting to be a writer. She was suddenly forced to wonder where that Madison had gone.

Months later, after a particular grueling day at work, Madison stopped at the drugstore to pick up a black composition book, the kind she used to journal in so many years ago. When she got home she poured a glass of wine and sat down with the empty book and put words on the page: *"Write fearlessly," he told me as he died.* And so I did.

Stuart

Living in the woods can get pretty lonely. At least I have Millie for company and to help keep my feet warm at night when she's willing. We had ol' Blue for a while, but he was always a curious mutt. Wandered onto a pack of unforgiving raccoons eating from the rubbish bin one night. They mauled him good, and despite Doc Jones' best work, we lost poor ol' Blue. Millie never seemed to be the same after he was gone. Thick as thieves those two were. Grew up together since the time they was nothing but babies. They use to sleep together on an old mattress I had on the back porch. Blue would lick Millie head to toe 'til she was sopping wet, and Millie would suck on Blue's fur the whole while. Had to get rid of that old mattress. Millie would stand on it all night meowing, as if she were trying raise Blue from the dead. When you don't have many folks in your life, any companion matters. Even if they are just animals.

For a while, I guess I took Blue's death pretty hard too. Millie's great company in her way, but Blue was my traveling buddy and my best friend. He would greet the day with me every morning, accompany me to work, where he would do his own fair share of the business, and lay down with me at night watching TV. His death left a pretty big hole in my life. And in my heart. I knew that place wasn't going to be filled by just any old dog, so I didn't really go looking for one. For a good while it was just Millie and me. That was until Stuart showed up.

I was walking the deep woods like I always do, marking trees for possible use as utility poles, which ain't an easy business. About maybe 1 in 70 trees is tall enough and straight enough. Of those, maybe half are the right strength and free of parasites. It was on one of these trips I found Stuart. The day was particularly balmy, so I didn't bring a jacket or anything. But as evening came, there was a chill in the air like the kind that speaks of Winter to come. I was hurrying to get home before dark when I happened upon a not unusual scene. A small gang of scrub jays were diving and pecking at something hidden in a patch of grass. One swooped in with a screech and darted its pointy beak at the unseen target. As soon as it turned to fly out of the patch, another one took its place. My curiosity got the best of me, I guess, because I just had to see what those birds were pestering.

    I knew right away what it was, but damned if it wasn't the cutest critter I pretty much ever saw. It was a baby crow. Not much more than a little black puffball with two big, shiny eyes and a tiny little beak. I have to admit, my gut response was to smash it under my boot. I'd like to believe that the reason was to put a poor suffering animal out of its misery, but I know better. It was because of habit gained from childhood when Will Achins and I tried to shoot just about any black bird we came across. "My dad says they're evil," Will always insisted. "Birds like that are spawned from the devil." He was quoting his father, who was known as a very pious man. When I told my own dad this, he'd scoffed. "Achins is backwards as backwards can be," he'd frown. It caused me great conflict that my dad and best friend did not agree, but in the end I made the mistake most kids make and sided with my friend. Will Achins and I killed a lot of birds when we was young and foolish. Something I feel guilty about to this very day. That feeling must've been what made me do what I did next.

    No momma in sight, and that fuzzy little black crow was screaming to wake the dead. Obviously, he was half starving. So I dug up a few handfuls of beetles and grubs and plopped them into that gaping pink mouth of his. When he was finally satisfied, I took off my flannel shirt and made a sling to carry him. I brought him home with me. I ended up calling him Stuart, after my uncle who died some time ago. He wasn't my favorite uncle or anything, but something about that crow reminded me of Uncle Stuart.

Stuart was happy-go-lucky from the beginning. Once he was well-feed on bugs and things, he would get into all sorts of shenanigans. But by far the biggest victim of his schemes was Millie. Millie was suspicious of Stuart from the start. Whenever Stuart came near her, she would ball up and hiss, smacking him on the top of his head. She never did it hard enough to stop him. Stuart delighted in sneaking up on her while she was sleeping. No small feat against an animal with super sensitive hearing. Somehow he managed to do it every single time. Then he'd do something like pull on her ear or snatch at her paw, sending her nearly flying to the ceiling. For his part, Stuart loved Millie. And he proved it one day in spades.

Millie was an indoor cat, and when she went missing one day, I knew something was not right. Stuart was a smart bird, and he developed all kinds of talents when he was with us. One of these was the ability to pick just about any lock. The latch on the skylight above the sink was a favorite. It took him about a week to figure it out. He had to hang upside down on the latch as he unfastened it with his beak before flying to a safe spot as the window slowly dropped open.

That first night he got it open was the night Millie went missing. I ran all around the outside of the house searching for her with a flashlight but couldn't find her. After a sleepless night, I spent half the next day looking for her. When I got back in the afternoon, I noticed Stuart had stuffed himself up onto the ledge of the skylight. He kept staring at me intently, then turning to his stare outside. Nothing could coax him from that spot. Not even a dish of his favorite food, popcorn. I couldn't help feeling like there was something he wanted to show me up there. The next day, still no Millie, and Stuart would not come down from the skylight. Every time I walked into the kitchen, he would call at me with that loud screeching sound he made when he was hungry.

"Come down if you want to eat," I said, not without annoyance. "I'm not bring it up there to you." But he kept doing it every time I walked by.

Finally I pulled out my foot ladder and climbed up to yank him down. When I tried to nab him, he nipped at my fingers. That was when I saw exactly what he wanted me to see. A terrified Millie was meowing desperately on a tree branch that stood just off the roof. I ran to the garage to get the big ladder and eased poor Millie out of that tree. Stuart watched the whole time from his spot in the skylight. He came down when I brought her into the house, practically dancing a jig around my feet. Never seen a happy crow in my life.

One thing I knew is I couldn't let Will Achins see old Stuart. No telling what Will would do to him. Will lived on the next farm over for most of my 68 years, about half a mile as the crow flies. He left once to attend Bible College but was gone for only 9 months before he decided it was not for him. Then he got married and was gone for another three years or so. He was pretty despondent when he got back after that. He never wanted to talk about it, so I never asked. Rumor was that his wife left him because she said he was too self-righteous. Whatever that means. Because of our individual circumstances, Will Achins and I both ended up living alone in our family homes. While I took solace in my animals and farming, Will found his peace in his Bible stories. We would meet occasionally to talk about things, mostly the past, but any real closeness we had as kids was pretty much long gone. As far as I knew, he still shot any black bird he came across. All the more reason to keep him far away from Stuart.

It worked for a time, refusing Will's invitations. I must've used every excuse in the book, and then some. I guess I thought if I could keep Will off long enough for Stuart to get big enough to be on his own, then we'd all be in the clear. But Spring soon turned to Summer, and Summer to Fall, with Winter just around the corner. Truth was,

Will and I needed each other come Winter. Winter's a long, cold spell. No one can survive it up here on their own. So around the end of November, as Millie was napping on the living room window with one eye on Stuart hunting for beetles in the front yard, I spied Will slowly making his way up the hill. As usual, he had his sidearm on his hip, an old, model 29 Smith & Wesson that had belonged to his father. It was hard to miss that distinctive long barrel. He carried it almost always for what he called "possible emergencies".

There was no time to hide Stuart so I hurried down the hill to cut Will off. He had a familiar, stern look on his face as I approached him, a look he inherited from his father.

"Ned," he greeted me with a nod.

"Will," I nodded back.

"Been some time," Will said before spitting chaw.

"Guess it has," I made a face. Never was a fan of chewing tobacco, or tobacco in general for that matter.

"Something the matter up here?" he said after a pause. He was trying to look past me at the house.

"Nothing unusual," I lied, to which he made a grunting noise.

"Gettin' near Winter," he said to the silence between us. "I'm guessin' you'll need help with the onions and squash."

"And you'll need help cleaning any moose you get," I returned. These were only a couple of the many duties we begrudgingly shared. Running a household in rough weather was life and death after all, and there was nothing for me to do but admit that Will and I needed each other's help. So we made a plan to harvest the following week, and Will slowly made his way back to his own home.

I did everything I could think of to coax Stuart to leave, short of chasing him into the forest. He was more than fully grown and smart enough to take care of himself. But it was clear to me he had no real desire to leave. Maybe he instinctively knew Winter was coming, and it would be easier to stay put with me. What I'd like to believe is that he enjoyed my company just about as much as I enjoyed his. Whatever the reason, try as I might, I could not persuade Stuart to go out on his own.

The day Will came walking back up the hill with his oversized Smith & Wesson, I was filled with a kind of dread. I decided that the only thing I could do was to be honest and upfront with him. To tell him about Stuart. I did not relish the thought of the lecture he was going to give me. One of his father's old fire-and-brimstone warnings of gloom and doom no doubt. He really had no idea of the truth of things. Stuart was about the furthest thing from evil in the entire world. Simple as that.

"Heya Will," I said as I met him on the hill.

"Heya," he said back.

"Listen, Will," I cleared my throat. "There's something I gotta–" And that was when the unthinkable happened.

I locked Stuart up in the house, using duct tape to secure the latches, including his favorite one on the skylight. He must've somehow figured out how to peel the tape off because the skylight was wide open and he was prancing around on the roof. Even though I had not yet seen Stuart myself, when I saw Will draw his gun I knew exactly what he was aiming for.

"No!" I yelled as I jumped forward to push his arm away. The .44 magnum rocketed loudly but harmlessly into the nearby forest.

"That's Stuart!" I shouted before he could aim again.

"It's what?" Will said with the most confused look I have ever seen on his face. I turned to look, but Stuart was nowhere to be seen.

"What were you shooting at?" I turned back to Will.

"A damn crow," he said with a frown.

"That's Stuart," I said again. "Stuart is my crow." And I told him the whole story, including the time he saved Millie.

We pulled onions and squash all day in silence. At dusk, I made us some leftover chicken and dumplings. We still didn't talk, only briefly to make plans for me to go over to Will's for the next set of Winter chores. Then Will walked back down the hill.

As for Stuart, all I could think was that the gunshot spooked him so much he must've fled into the forest. He didn't come back the next day, or the next week. Or the next month.

Winter came on quick, and lasted a good long time. Stuart still didn't come. I worried the whole season, and couldn't help thinking the worst.

Sometime the following Spring, Millie and I were relaxing in the living room when she sprang up to the skylight. She meowed loudly as she stared at something in the yard. I went over to look at what it was, and I really couldn't believe my eyes. Stuart was there, and he had two smaller crows with him. Had he come to introduce us to his family.

10

"Ten years old. The Big Ten. Tenarooski. Double Digits. The might one zero!" George's dad rambled.

There was a time when George enjoyed his dad's antics, but more and more they just annoyed him. He gave a pretend little laugh in hopes that his dad would stop.

"Ten-diddle-end!" As usual his dad had to throw in one last zinger. George willed himself not to roll his eyes.

George was an only child, so he had no reference for what it was like to turn ten. He just knew he wanted it to be awesome.

"Georgie," his mom called.

"It's George!" he said disdainfully. If he could get his mom to stop calling him "Georgie" it would be one step closer to the best birthday ever.

"I'm going to ride my bike to school today," George didn't even ask. "By myself." It would be his first time riding alone.

"Okay," his dad said after he and his mom exchanged a surprised look.

It was February and cold, but George didn't care. The wind blew through his hair as he drifted down the hill. It was the most freedom he had ever experienced in his young life, and he loved it. He wanted more of that feeling.

At school, George raised his hand in class five times and got called on three times. Two of those time his answers were correct. Later his teacher, Ms. Wilmington, complimented him for putting forth more effort in class. It felt really good to hear this complement from a teacher that normally seemed to ignore him.

For first recess, no one wanted to be the goalie, so George stepped into the net. Something inside him clicked. He had no problem deflecting every ball that came at him, and his team ended up winning the match 2–0. At lunch they served his favorite meal: little, round, cheese pizzas with syrupy peaches and chocolate pudding in the can. It felt as if the lunch lady had prepared it just for him.

Lunch recess turned out to be the most fun of all. George's best friend found a black ant mound. Together they stacked sticks on top of it to create an ant fort. The ants swarmed over the sticks, clearly agitated by their presence. George found a red ant, the large kind that have a nasty bite. He scooped it up with a piece of paper and dropped it into the middle of the fort. The black ants turned their ire onto the red ant. It was quickly overwhelmed. Ant War Recess was proclaimed the best recess ever.

Before the end of the day, the class sang Happy Birthday to George and they ate cupcakes provided by his mother. They were white cake with chocolate frosting, George's favorite. To top it off, it was Friday, so the teacher gave them no homework. As George left for the day, he did a little dance. He could not remember having a better day at school.

Then Ralph Mendel met him in front of the school. Ralph was the resident, sixth-grade bully.

"Nice bike," Ralph said before pushing George to the ground. "Here's your birthday present." Ralph punched George 10 times on various parts of his body.

"Now *I* want a birthday present," Ralph sneered as he stood over George. "Gimme your bike."

"HEY!" someone yelled, and Ralph took off like a shot. It was the crossing guard. He ran over to George and helped him off the ground.

At home, George cried in his mother's arms as his father called the principal.

"I just wanted the perfect birthday…" George whimpered.

"Don't let it get to you honey," his mother said softly. "We still have the weekend to make it the best birthday ever."

His parents went out of their way to do just that, taking George to an arcade, a soda fountain, and a sci-fi double feature. He had a great time.

But despite it all, the thing George would always remember most about his tenth birthday was being punched 10 times by Ralph Mendel.

The Rainbow

A rainbow appeared in the sky. It was big, and bold, and beautiful, as rainbows often are.

Because it was new to the world, the rainbow knew very little. It did not know that its life was finite and would soon end.

A jaded storm cloud, who was jealous of the rainbow's colors, decided to tease the rainbow.

"You can live forever," the storm cloud smirked. "But only If you follow the horizon until you touch the sun." This, of course, was impossible.

The rainbow, who did not know that the sun was millions of miles away, tried to chase it. She stretched as hard as she could into the distance which caused her colors to slowly fade.

The rainbow could hear the storm cloud cackling in the distance as she slowly disappeared.

• • •

The next day, a second rainbow appeared.

The bitter storm cloud played his trick again.

The second rainbow also vanished into the ether.

• • •

The storm cloud tricked countless rainbows this way until one day a mountaintop noticed what he was doing.

"Stop!" the mountaintop boomed. Few elements on the planet were as old and wise as the mountaintop. He immediately saw through the storm cloud's ruse.

"Come and rest yourself on my mountain," he said to the newest rainbow. "And I will tell you tales of hope."

The rainbow joined the mountaintop, who told her the truth of rainbows: "It is true that a rainbow's life is short. But it is equally true that their majestic beauty is unmatched upon this earth. This is what makes you truly unique."

This rainbow lasted much longer than the others. And when she finally faded, she left the world with joy as opposed to the fear that the storm cloud inspired in the others. This left the hapless storm cloud wanting.

As the storm cloud's jealousy turned to sadness and heavy rain, he also disappeared from the world. His tears brought forth lush greenery upon the mountaintop, but most importantly he never again bothered another rainbow.

Longing for the Moon

The moon was lonely. It was a hard job lighting up the night sky while everyone else was sleeping.

One day the moon took up singing in order to pass the time. She sang songs about boredom and loneliness. She sang songs about love and loss. She even sang songs about joy and happiness that she longed to feel.

A passing cloud heard the moon's melancholy songs and stopped to listen. The moon's song touched him so deeply that he began to weep, which formed into rain. The rain washed over the earth. It made the earth feel fresh and new.

"Thank you," the earth said to the cloud.

"Thank the moon," the cloud replied. "Her songs made me cry. And every time I cry I feel lighter," the cloud said as he floated away.

The earth became very interested in the moon. But the earth was shy and could not get himself to address her. He watched her sing from afar.

Eventually the earth fell in love with the moon.

It went on for centuries this way, the moon singing her songs and the earth quietly listening.

Then unexpectedly, the moon stopped singing. The earth was confused and grew anxious. Why did the moon end her beautiful song?

"Moon," the earth called. "Oh moon."

The moon did not answer. For whatever reason, she had given up.

The earth was filled with longing. Why had he never spoken to her? Why did he never tell her how beautiful her songs were?

Sadly the longing turned to regret, and the earth was left to wonder for the rest of eternity what might have been.

The Walk

A boy decided to walk around the world.

He left a note for his mother:

> *"Goodbye. I will always love you. I hope to see you again someday.*
>
> *Love,*
> *Your Son*

Before he left, he visited his father's grave.

"I'm leaving, Dad," he said sadly. "And I don't know if I will ever come back."

As he turned to go, the boy heard a familiar voice.

"Then I will go with you," the voice said.

"Who's there?" the boy asked.

"It's me," the voice answered. "Your father."

"But I can't see you," the boy said.

"No," his father said. "You will never be able to see me. Just know that I will always be with you, wherever you go. And when you need me, I will do what I can to help."

The boy did not believe his father. His father had, after all, left him once. What was to stop him from doing so again.

"Okay," was all the boy could say.

The first days were very hard. The boy was not used to walking so much, and he tired out easily. He quickly became lonely, and when he tried to talk to his father, there was no answer. Worst of all, the little bit of food he brought with him ran out quickly.

The boy had only been gone for a few days and was laying down to sleep one night when it started to rain. At a loss as to what to do, the boy curled into a ball and began to cry.

Suddenly he heard a loud cracking sound. Terrified, he looked up to see the tree branches above him bending into the shape of a shelter. Soon he was nice and dry.

"Dad?" he said softly as he drifted into exhausted slumber.

After a few days with nothing to eat, the boy felt as if he was going to collapse. He sat down on a rock, staring into space. Just when he was seriously considering eating some dry leaves and grass, a thought occurred to him: *Follow the birds.*

"Birds?" he mumbled in bewilderment.

The boy nearly fell off the rock when a bird swooped over his head with a piercing chirp. He turned to see a few more birds fluttering about in the nearby woods. In a daze of hunger, he stumbled after them. Not far into the bramble, a small gang of birds were nibbling on large purple berries. There were millions of the plump, juicy fruits dotting the surrounding greenery. The boy ravenously shoveled handfuls of sticky berries into his mouth. By the time he was done, his face and hands were stained a deep purple.

So it went on this way. Whenever the boy had a need, he was provided for in some mysterious way.

Eventually the boy grew into a young man. Life on the run grizzled him. It was so long since he had contact with other people, that he could not imagine being with anyone. It had also been quite a while since he received any help from his father. The older he got, the less help he seemed to need.

Then he had a dream:

His father appeared to him and said, "The time has come to go home."

"But I don't want to," said the young man. "In fact, I don't really care if I never see home again."

His father gave a frustrated sigh.

"Very well," he said. "But I can only help you one more time, and then it will finally be time for me to rest."

More time passed, and the boy was fine. He had learned how to find his own food, make his own shelter, and keep his own way. He was very self-sufficient.

But he got reckless.

He climbed mountains without ropes, rode rapids without a boat, and chased dangerous animals, like cougars and coyotes, for fun. In his frenzy, he got hurt more than once. He stopped paying attention to his surrounds. As a result, one day he inadvertently fell into a deep, empty well.

Fortunately, the fall did not cause him any broken bones, but the sides of the well were much too smooth to scale. There was no way out.

"Dad? Dad?" the young man called. There was no answer.

Night fell, and still the young man was trapped in the well.

"Dad?! Dad?!" he yelled into the dark sky. Still no answer.

At a loss, the young man laid his back against the sidewall of the well and fell asleep.

The next day, he ate the last of what food he had, drank what water was left. He waited and waited and waited, but nothing happened.

Three days passed and the boy was desperate. He tried over and over to scramble up the sides of the well. Each time, he merely slid back down to the bottom. He pounded his fists on the sides of the well until his hands stung.

The young man yelled: "You said you would help me one more time! You said you would! I knew you were lying to me! I knew you would leave me again when I needed you the most!!"

Suddenly a face appeared over the side. The young man could not make out who it was.

"Dad?" he called.

A rope was lowered to him, and he slowly climbed out of his hole. He lay on the ground, panting as he was handed a canteen full of cool water. He drank until he could drink no more. When he was offered food, he was able to focus on who had saved him.

"Mom?" he said with great surprise.

"It's time to come home," she smiled.

By the time they got home, the young man could think of nothing but sleeping in his own bed.

By the time they got home, his father was able to rest in peace.

By the time he got home, the boy was a child once again.

Pecker

Al moved into his parents' house shortly after his mother died. Al was an only child, and his last remaining family were distant in blood, geography and heart. He was an unintentional loner, and now that he was retired, he had no real friends. He never had children, and his wife left him many years ago.

The family home was a 100-year-old Craftsman nestled in the middle of a small town. Its most distinguishing feature was the siding which Al's father had proudly claimed was the original wood. It was overdue for a sanding and repaint, so that was the first thing Al planned to do.

No sooner did Al purchase supplies and pull the ladder out of the garage when he noticed a track of small holes running along the southern end of the house.

"Damn peckers," he muttered angrily. He counted the damaged boards. There were at least 25 that would need to be replaced. He checked the rest of the house. Thankfully the other walls had been spared, but Al knew it was only a matter of time before the woodpecker came back to ruin some more wood. He might even bring some friends.

Al used an old shirt and some pants to make a scarecrow. He stuffed them with socks and used a deflated basketball for the face. He watched from the screened porch as the offending woodpecker flitted into the oak tree just outside the backyard. It sized up the scarecrow, which was standing close to its holes. It gave a loud twitter and vanished into the woods.

"Stupid pecker," Al chuckled.

A few weeks later, Al woke to an unmistakable sound. Half asleep, he stumbled into the yard where he caught a flickering glimpse of black and white. The woodpecker chittered at him from the nearby oak tree. Several fresh holes were bored into the side of the house. The useless scarecrow drooped sadly.

"Shoo pecker, shoo!!" Al shouted and waved his arms as he ran at the bird. The startled woodpecker darted into the woods. This was his tactic for the next few days, until he realized it was impossible to be ready at all times to chase off the woodpecker. Many more holes littered the wood siding.

Exacerbated once more, Al went to the local hardware store where they recommended plastic owls. He took a half dozen home and lined the eaves with his small army of the stern faced statues. The effect lasted about a month, but the woodpecker eventually returned to its drilling. Al was so shocked and surprised to hear that horrible sound, that he nearly tripped on his way out the backdoor. The woodpecker bolted when Al appeared. Al's eyes followed it as it landed on top of the head of the nearest plastic owl. It was the perfect vantage point for the bird to see the entire yard.

"Blasted pecker!" Al shook his fist. He now counted 52 damaged boards. "Fuckin' pecker!!"

The next day Al went into his father's gun closet. He picked out one of the shotguns. He meticulously cleaned it with oil and a rag before loading two large shells with a heavy click. Al had reached a threshold that all of us walk at one time in our lives, a place somewhere between madness and desperation where we are apt to perform uncharacteristic or even reprehensible acts. He carried the shotgun onto the porch and spied the woodpecker creeping along the side of the house. It was unafraid, shifting its body to a fresh board before beginning again its relentless hammering. Al leveled the gun and aimed it toward the hapless bird. His finger danced on the trigger as his teeth gnashed in his mouth.

Suddenly a light shone in his eyes causing him to blink and lower the gun. Al shielded his eyes with his hands and tried to see from where the light was coming. He caught a glimpse of a young boy in the window next door. The boy was holding up a hand mirror and using the reflection of the sun to aim a beam of light into Al's face. When the boy realized Al saw him, he gasped and disappeared behind a curtain.

Seeing the boy sparked a childhood memory. When he was young, Al loved to watch the birds in the backyard. He would put out feeders and water bowls. He even made a list of the ones he saw: bluebird, mockingbird, blue jay, robin, oriole, cardinal, tanager, junco, chickadee, and his favorite… woodpecker. When he was a kid, Al would have done anything to protect those birds.

Al watched as the woodpecker found a new spot on the side of the house and pounded away with its sharp beak. He shook his head, rubbed the back of his neck, and took a deep breath.

"God blessed pecker," he muttered before stepping back into the house.

Man and the Devil

One day, a man met the Devil who was nothing like what he imagined the Devil would be like.

"What's with the fire and brimstone thing anyway?" the man asked.

"I don't do brimstone anymore. It's too destructive."

"More destructive than fire?" the man frowned. "I find that hard to believe." And so the Devil made a wager with the man. He bet the man that brimstone would burn down more forest than fire. The man laughed. Surely fire would consume a whole forest long before brimstone caused a spark.

Together they went into the forest where the man watched the Devil set his brimstone in a small pile of leaves. The man tossed his fire into another pile of leaves. As soon as the man did so, the Devil whisked up a wind and blew the fire out. Meanwhile the brimstone caused a spark in the leaves. The spark became a flame. The flame quickly burned down the entire forest.

"Now you must pay me for the wager," the Devil grinned.

"Take what you must," the man said.

"You must choose what I will take from you," the Devil said in that way he has. "Your dog, your wife, your daughter, or yourself."

Without hesitation, the man replied, "Take me."

Immediately the Devil took the man with him to Hell, but

something strange happened. As soon as the man touched the fires of Hell, everything around him turned cold. The coldness quickly spread until the fires of hell were nothing more than black smoke.

"What have you done?" the Devil wailed, for the spreading cold was beginning to hurt him too.

"It's not what I did, it's what you did," smiled the man. "By bringing me here, you ruined yourself."

"But how?" the Devil asked in anguish.

"The choices you gave me," the man said. "My wife left me long ago because I cheated on her with other women. My dog ran away because I beat him merciless. And my son died of cancer just six months ago."

A look of horrible understanding darkened the Devil's face.

"My heart has grown colder than any ice storm," the man spat. "Bringing me here was the worst thing you could do."

The Devil collapsed onto a rock, his head in his hands. Who was this man? How had he not known him?

"I'll tell you what," the man whispered into the Devil's ear. "Let's talk about another wager." For the man was far from done. He had much bigger plans, and he would not stop until he became the Devil himself.

The Social Worker

Mandy was a Social Worker fresh out of college. In school she was known as a go-getter and had fast-tracked her way to a good job with the county. She was excited to finally be helping people, which was her career goal since she was six years old.

Mandy was given Sam, a seven-year-old boy with severe behavior problems at school. Sam attacked kids without provocation and absolutely refused to do his school work. He had even scratched and kicked a teacher.

Mandy did her best to diagnose Sam: Attention Deficit Hyperactivity Disorder without ruling out of Oppositional Defiant Disorder. Then she got to work.

Sam was difficult to talk to, because he would not answer questions. Sometimes, he came to session soiled with urine and feces. Mandy would have to take him to the school nurse who would huff loudly as she cleaned Sam as best she could.

"You know this is a sign of abuse," the nurse said one day in an angry tone. "You're supposed to report abuse."

Mandy tried to ask questions of Sam in order to assess for abuse. As usual, Sam would not cooperate. He only wanted to make the chess board piece dance around the room with magic ponies.

Mandy asked her supervisor what she should do. He suggested a home visit, if the family would allow it.

"You'll learn a lot from meeting the parents," he said. "Things you don't necessarily want to know."

It took several attempts, but Mandy eventually spoke with Sam's grandmother. She seemed pleasant enough.

"Sure, come on over! And bring some Dr. Pepper." Mandy wasn't sure if this was a request or a demand.

Mandy dutifully bought a six-pack of Dr. Pepper and headed south of the city. Houses turned to apartments. Apartments turned to vacant lots and abandoned buildings. Sam's "house" turned out to be a dilapidated trailer. Mandy wasn't sure she was in the right place, but the number on the lot matched the address she had written down. She opened the gate, walked up to the trailer, and knocked on the door. A short but large woman popped out and gave her a gap-toothed grin.

"You must be the Social Worker," she said. She spied the Dr. Pepper and eagerly clutched it in her hands. "Wonderful!" she smiled. "Come on in!"

Mandy stepped into the trailer. It was filthy, tattered, worn, and permeated with a horrific smell. There was only one seat which the grandmother offered to Mandy. A couple of potatoes were boiling on the stove in the tiny kitchenette just a few feet away.

"Who the hell is that?" a voice boomed from the back of the trailer. An elderly man with a scraggly white beard stepped out of the shadows.

"Shut up and go back to sleep!" the grandmother grimaced. He waved his hand in annoyance and did just that.

"My husband," she rolled her eyes.

Mandy didn't even have to ask any questions before Sam's grandmother, whose name was Laurie, spilled her story.

"I have mental illness myself. They call it manic and I take like five different medications." She shoved the bottles at Mandy. "My husband, the asshole, has cancer and will probably die any day. He doesn't get treated because he has no insurance and he's too damn lazy to get some. Anyway he's here illegally so it's not like he can get any. We don't get along too well, me and the old man, but he's all I got, so I don't have the heart to kick him out." She itched under her breast and that was when Mandy saw she had no bra.

Laurie caught her noticing and laughed. "I haven't owned a bra in ten years, if that's what you're looking at. They're too fucking expensive! Four of us live off of my social security, 800 dollars a month, and it's not dang near enough. Saw you looking at the potatoes too. We can't afford no meat. I don't know when the last time I had a steak was. And I see the look in your eye. You're not the first *social worker* to come here you know. You're number five, and they all do the same thing and ask the same questions. My daughter may be a retard, but she does the best she can with that boy. She loves that boy to death. We all love that boy more than anything and would do anything for him. If you take him away from us, you take him away from his home and his family. And you take away the only good thing we have in this world. There might as well be no reason for us to live—" She stopped because she was crying too hard to speak.

Mandy suddenly felt like an intruder. Everything she knew about what a family should be was torn apart in less than five minutes. *If you take him away from us, you take him away from his home and family. And you take away the only good thing we have.* It was something she imagined her own mother saying about her. "I'm not going to take Sam away," she said quietly and excused herself.

The next day, Mandy called in sick. Her boss was angry because she had only been working the job for four weeks. So she quit.

Her mother was shocked but elated when Mandy decided to go to medical school. She was still very young and if she kept on track she would be a doctor by the time she was thirty. Mandy wasn't even sure she wanted to be a doctor. She thought she wanted to help people, but wasn't even sure about that any more. All she could think of was to get lost in school and books for as long as she could.

RV

Mort bought an old school bus for about 800 dollars at a junk lot. It was gutted, and the engine was gone, but none of this mattered to Mort. After a lifetime of fixing cars of every imaginable shape and size, the RV was exactly what he wanted.

Mort lost his wife the year before, just six months after he retired. Not knowing what to do without her, he ended up selling everything they had, including their home of 23 years. The memories were just too painful to bear.

His brother, Bart, let Mort live in his garage while Mort rebuilt the old bus.

"Whadaya gonna do?" Bart would ask everyday with a beer in his hand. Mort would shake his head and get back to work.

He started by putting in a small bathroom and kitchen. The plumbing was tricky because he had never done it before, but looking at a few diagrams online was all he needed to do to figure it out. He ran electrical lines for the stove and various light fixtures. The biggest undertaking was rebuilding the engine. He had to enlist the help of his reluctant brother who groused the entire time.

"I ain't the one who was a mechanic," Bart would groan.

Last came the dining room and the bedroom. Mort spent quite a bit of time decorating these, the way he knew his wife would have if she was still alive. The whole thing had taken no more than three months.

Mort said goodbye to the place where he was born, the place

where he had grown up, the place he had lived for his entire life. He had no real plans other than to drive away.

"Whadaya gonna do?" his Bart asked for the umpteenth time. Mort didn't answer, because he didn't really have an answer. He stepped aboard the bus and turned the key. The engine roared. He pulled it in gear and drove away with the image of his brother, beer in hand, in the rear view mirror.

The road for several hundred miles was empty. Mort drove in silence because the radio was receiving no signal. The rumble of the engine was soothing, and staring at the long stretch of road brought him a feeling of peace he had not felt since before his wife's death. It was not long before boredom set in, and then the thoughts.

Suddenly Mort was crying like he never had before.

A Boy and His Dog

Joe found Digger cowering under a car one morning when he was on his paper route. Digger was a chubby pup with puffy fur and sad eyes. Joe scooped him up and placed him in his paper route bag. Digger snuggled up to the newspapers and fell asleep during the ride home.

Joe named him Digger because the first night he left him in the backyard alone, Digger dug up his mom's chili pepper plants. Joe's mom nearly kicked the dog out of the yard, but even she could not resist his puppy whine.

Digger grew up fast, and Joe took him on his paper route every day. Someone said that the dog looked part husky so Joe attached his leash to the bike handlebars and let Digger pull him through the streets.

"I would never do that to you," scoffed an old man who was walking his Chihuahua one morning.

Because you don't have a dog like Digger, Joe wanted to say, but was too respectful to do so.

Digger had some bad habits. He loved to roll in cat poop when he found it. It didn't help that Joe egged him on by yelling "Go get 'em! Go get 'em!" whenever Digger saw a cat.

Joe was a nature lover and went hiking outdoors whenever he could. He took long walks to the local lake and explored the wooded areas near a winding river. He collected snails and tadpoles to put in a pond he dug in his backyard.

Digger was his constant companion on these trips. He grew

bigger than a German Shepard, and was a loyal watchdog. When a spindly pit bull threatened Joe, Digger took up the challenge. He leapt onto the muscular mutt with a snarl, knocking both of them into the lake. The fight ended in a dripping wet draw, but in Joe's eyes the victory belonged to faithful Digger.

When Joe got older and bolder, he tricked his parents into believing he was spending the night at a friend's house. Instead he slept at the lake. Sleeping bag in hand, he trekked into the wilderness and camped on the side of a hill. Digger came along of course.

It was a restless night as Joe shivered from the cold. He feared attack by either a wild animal or a psycho-killer. Digger could not sleep either. He would periodically run off to investigate strange sounds.

Near dawn, Digger ran down the other side of the hill with a growl in his throat. Joe jumped up to see what he was charging toward. In the clearing below, an alert coyote stood. Digger was nearly nose-to-nose with it. When it noticed Joe, it scrambled into the bushes. Joe did not want to think of what would have happened if Digger had not been there to protect him.

Time passed and Joe became busy with high school, and life in general. He traded his paper route for a job at Taco Bell, and his bike for a cherry-red Nissan Sentra. He would go months without walking Digger.

Digger, being the dog he was, did not take this lying down. He figured out how to open the backyard fence, and went to look for Joe. He jogged the five miles to the lake, careful to look both ways before crossing the streets, just as Joe had taught him. He charged into the river, chasing guppies and tadpoles. He knocked over a trash can and gobbled down some old cake. He chased a flock of quacking ducks into the lake. It was like old times, except no Joe.

After a day or two, Digger found his way home. About once a month, he found a way out and went on another solo adventure. After a few days, he would come back home to find Joe.

When Joe finally went away to college, Digger grew anxious. He whined and barked all the time. Never had he felt so alone.

One day, Digger made up his mind. He all but knocked the fence down and charged straight to the lake. He was never going to come back. When weeks had passed with no Digger, Joe was devastated. He felt guilty for having neglected Digger for so long.

As for Digger, he met a pack of stray dogs. They lived together at the lake where they caused all sorts of mayhem. Digger thought about Joe sometimes, and at those times he could not help but feel a bit lonely. But in a certain light, if he squinted just right, he thought he could almost see Joe walking on a nearby hill. At those moments, it was almost as if Joe had never left him.

The Albatross

"Let's fly to the North," an albatross said to his wife one day.

"You know I don't like the North," his wife scowled. "And anyway it's almost time to build our nest so that I can lay our egg."

The albatross did not like the way she said *our egg*.

"I tell you what," he said. "I'll take a trip alone to the North and come back in a few days to finish the nest."

"Don't be ridiculous," his wife snapped.

That night, when his wife was sleeping, the albatross lifted silently into the air and drifted like a passenger jet to the North. It was a long journey, and he had a lot of time to think. His thoughts were not pleasant. He thought about how his wife nagged him, a lot. He thought about how she often told him his ideas were ridiculous, about how she never wanted to do anything fun or exciting anymore. He thought about how she made fun of him when he was dreaming about something new, like going to the North.

"Why can't I experience new things?" the albatross grumbled to himself. "There's a whole world out there that I am missing out on because of her."

As soon as he got to the North, the albatross was amazed at how different everything was. Even the birds were unique. Some were tiny and brown. Others were jet black and pointy. Still, others were as bright and shiny as the blue sky. He stopped to talk to a portly grey bird with a chest dappled in iridescent feathers.

"Hello," he called to the grey bird. "What kind of bird are you?"

"Say what?" said the grey bird, obviously confused.

"What kind of bird are you?" the albatross asked again in the friendliest way he could. He tried to say the words more slowly in hopes that this strange bird would understand.

"The kind of bird that thinks you're a dumbass," the plump bird said before fluttering clumsily away with its tiny wings. The albatross looked at his own massive wings and was suddenly thankful for being an albatross.

The next bird he came across was a sleek black one. He found it in the middle of a grass clearing, pecking at the bloody remains of a small animal's head.

"Excuse me," the albatross addressed the dark bird. He was much more cautious and polite this time. "Can you please tell me what kind of bird you are?"

The black bird turned its sharp eyes toward the albatross. It cocked its head from side to side as if measuring the albatross.

"Albatross, right," the black bird said in a throaty voice.

"Excuse me?" the albatross responded, because he wasn't sure if it was a statement or a question.

"You're an albatross," the bird said not unpleasantly.

"Yes I am," the albatross relaxed a little. At least this bird was not calling him names.

"Tell you what," the bird said. "If you go to the lake over there and catch us a fish, I'll answer all your questions."

It was extremely easy for the albatross to swoop over the lake and scoop up a large fish. This was, after all, what an albatross did best.

He shared it with the black bird as promised, and the bird willingly answered all his questions.

"I'm a crow," he said between bites of fish.

"What is this place?" the albatross continued.

"New York, New York, of course," the crow pronounced. "The city so nice they named it twice. The city that never sleeps. Center of the universe. Capital of the free world. The Great Melting Pot. The Big Apple. A hell of a town!"

The albatross could not help but feel like this crow fellow had a habit of repeating things he heard.

"You're a long way from home, albatross," the crow said as it preened.

"I came here to get away," the albatross said sadly.

"Away from what?" the crow asked.

"I'm not sure," the albatross sighed. The two departed from each other, but not before the crow told the albatross what were the best sights to see. So the albatross took a tour of places like the Empire State building, Broadway, and the Brooklyn Bridge. Wherever he went, people would point at him and talk about how unusual he looked. Clearly he was a long way from home.

The albatross almost had his fill of New York, especially the people, and was ready to leave when he visited the last destination on the crow's list: the Statue of Liberty. The fact that it looked like a giant green person immediately turned off the albatross. He was just about to start for home when he saw in the distance, sitting on the top of the torch of the humongous green lady, a beautiful brown bird. Intrigued, he flew over to land close to the mysterious bird. Its bold, brown feathers were gorgeous. Its big, yellow eyes were dazzling. It had a massive beak and enormous curled talons. The albatross had never seen such an amazing bird.

"Hello," he said shyly. The brown bird turned its head slowly to him, but did not respond.

"I'm an albatross," he said. "What kind of bird are you?"

"Hawk," the bird said, and the albatross could tell by the voice that the bird was a lady.

"You're…" He wanted to say beautiful, but he couldn't get it out.

"Follow me," the hawk said, and suddenly glided into the air like a cloud. The albatross joined her, and they danced high in the sky together, so high that the cars the people rode in looked like ants. The albatross and the hawk did not speak. There was no need for words. He felt his heart beat for her, and he could hear hers beating for him.

They spent the night together telling each other stories of what it was like to be a hawk and what it was like to be an albatross. But when morning came, the albatross was distant. The hawk asked him to fly with her again, but the albatross refused.

"I have to go home," he said in a somber tone. Because she was a hawk, the albatross could not tell what her look meant. He liked to think she was disappointed, but who could say. He said goodbye and began the long journey home. It was not an easy trip. After leaving New York, he was greeted with a violent storm. Then a man tried to shoot him, but fortunately he was a terrible aim. After landing for a rest near a farmyard, a cat jumped him. He was able to beat it off with his enormous wings but not without suffering some nasty scratches. The albatross was a bit ruffled by the time he reached his wife, who was understandably surprised to see him.

"I thought you were dead," she said with no real emotion.

"No, I'm alive," he answered, also with no real emotion.

"Well," she huffed. "I have bad news for you."

"You do?"

"I have a new mate." Hearing these words caused a feeling of joy inside him that the albatross had not felt since he was a young bird, since before he met his wife. It was a feeling he enjoyed very much.

"Oh really," he tried to sound disappointed.

"Yeah," she said. "I'm really sorry," she added, moving aside to show him two shiny eggs in her nest.

"No, it's okay," he said a little too quickly. "I probably would have done the same thing."

She gave him one of her usual angry looks.

"I mean, if I thought you were dead, I mean," he stumbled.

The albatross said a hasty last goodbye to his ex-wife and flew into the sky, resolving never to return to this cold and dismal place. As he headed away, he thought about where he should go. Maybe the East, or the West, or somewhere else in the North. Wherever he decided to go, he could not wait to discover the wonders these places held.

The Man on the Moon

A man decided to move to the moon.

When he first got to the moon, it was an interesting place to be: all the weird moon rocks, the grey powdery sand, the massive craters, that odd cheesy smell. But all of this got old pretty quick.

Soon, the man felt lonely. The loneliness got so bad that he started talking to the rocks. He gave them names like Trudy and Vincent, Albert and Camille. Then, one day, as if by magic, the rocks began to talk back.

Trudy sounded like a flirty Southern Belle, calling him names like "shuga" and "dumplin." Vincent was an angry New Yorker who used the word "fuck" for emphasis. Albert was the smart guy who valued reason above all else. And Camille was timid and shy.

On one particularly excruciating night, when the man could not get warm, it was rough-and-tumble Vincent who brought up what everyone else was thinking.

"We gotta get the fuck off the goddamn moon!" he said.

Unfortunately, not even Albert could come up with an idea on how to do so. That was when the man came to a decision. He once heard a rumor that there was a doorway on the dark side of the moon that would take you anywhere you wanted to go. So he picked up the rocks and started walking toward the dark side of the moon.

"Do you realize how absurd that sounds?" protested Albert.

While the man agreed, he knew he had to do something. He could not very while sit around on the moon talking to rocks forever.

After several days of walking, the man came to the largest crater he had ever seen. It was huge even by moon standards.

"I do declare, that is one enormous crater!" Trudy gasped.

There was nothing to do but walk around it. Hours and hours later, when he reached the other side, the man sat down to rest. Truth be told, he was dead tired and ready to give up. Chances were when he got to the dark side of the moon he would freeze and die anyway. It was not supposed to be a good place to be.

He took the rocks out of his pocket and lined them up in the dust. Everyone was quiet for a long time. Of all rocks, it was Camille who finally spoke: "If you don't try, you will never know," she simply said.

No one could argue with that, not even Albert.

Once again the man stuffed his pants with the rocks and continued to make his way to the dark side of the moon. It was rough going. Many times, he wanted to give up, lie in the dust, and wait for whatever end would come.

Each time Camille said the same thing, "If you don't try, you will never know."

42 days after he started, the man arrived at the dark side of the moon. He collapsed to the ground with utter exhaustion. Suddenly, he was consumed by a blazing light.

When his eyes adjusted, he could just make out a couple running ahead of him, laughing as they danced together into the light. As they embraced, he realized they were exactly what he imagined Trudy and Vincent would look like if they were real people. Next, he saw the form of Albert, who was holding a large stack of books. He gave the man a wink through his horn rimmed glasses before marching slowly into the light. And last, he saw the beautiful figure of Camille standing next to him. Her golden hair was shimmering in the brightness. Her sky blue eyes sparkled as she smiled at him.

"We're home," she said softly as she took his hand and brought him deeper into the light.

The Wind

A wind blew in from the East.

The air from the West thought the wind smelled funny. It refused to talk to the wind.

The wind tried to strike up a conversation about sports or favorite animals or exotic places. The westerly air continued to refuse to respond.

The wind from the East got an idea.

Everyone likes music, the wind thought. *I will make some music for the air.*

The wind blew through the branches of the trees to create a soft rhythm. The wind whistled over the rocks in a stream. The wind fluttered through the tall reeds of grass in a meadow. The wind blasted through a small canyon near the hills. The stubborn air still ignored the wind.

The wind did not give up. The wind ruffled through the feathers of dozens and dozens of birds of all sizes, encouraging them to add to his music with their own distinct sounds. The wind rushed into the sky, and back down to the ground at a fierce speed creating a cacophonous symphony of atmospheric sound.

This tremendous effort exhausted the wind. Soon it faded into nothing more than a light breeze. Just like that, the wind was gone.

And because it no longer had the wind to feed it, the air ceased to exist as well.

Chicken Suit Larry

That's what they called him: Chicken Suit Larry. Of course his name wasn't Larry. It was Dan, and he loved comic books, but only the ones nobody else read like *Madame Mirage* and *Axe Cop*. He worked for the Chicken Shack on Highway 9 whose claim to fame was deep-fried chicken gizzards and spicy macaroni salad. Dan was the chicken man, the guy who came to work dressed in a big yellow chicken suit and waved a sign on the corner that read "Chicken Lickin' 'Licious!" Dan was a shy guy, and no one at work knew his name, so the kitchen staff had taken to calling him Chicken Suit Larry.

Like most people who barely made minimum wage, Dan hated his job. He did it to pay the bills, which most of the time it did not. In the early days, he sometimes got free food, but truth be told, he did not like the food he was selling. The chicken was dry from having been frozen and refrozen, heated and reheat. The macaroni salad had a weird pasty taste that coated his mouth. Also, his obnoxious coworkers did horrific things to the food. Once he spied the fry cook using a sandwich wrapper to wipe his butt. He and the order cook laughed hysterically as the fry cook stuck it back on the pile of wrappers. That was when Dan vowed never to eat the Chicken Shack food again. To get through the day, sometimes Dan would fantasize that the sign he was holding actually read: "Worst Chicken in Town". It would definitely be an accurate sign.

The only good thing about his job was the mysterious lady who stood catty-corner from him. She was dressed in an aquamarine Statue of Liberty robe. She was the most beautiful woman Dan had ever seen. She had blazing, auburn hair, alabaster skin that glowed in the sunshine, and an hourglass figure that showed through the baggy robe. She held a torch in one hand, and in the other, a sign for a loan company called Freedom Financial that read, "Scorchin' Good Deals!" Dan liked to think her name was Lady Lana Liberty.

Dan often daydreamed about meeting her. A typical scenario involved her suddenly becoming trapped against the loan building by a car or a bus. Dan would swoop in like a hawk to save her. A gathered crowd would cheer loudly as he pulled her to safety. Overcome with gratitude, she would kiss him and whisper in his ear, "My hero!" just like in his comic books. Dan knew how corny it sounded, but it helped to break up the monotony of his day.

One day, a man dressed as an ice cream cone with a big red cherry on his head appeared a few doors down for Lady Lana. His sign was for the newly-opened Cow Creamery and it read, "Mooving Good Times!"

It's not even a clever slogan, Dan thought angrily.

He watched in horror for the next few days as Ice Cream Man eventually worked his way over to Lana. He smiled at her and struck up a conversation. From this distance, it was too hard to see her face, so Dan could not tell how she felt about him. But Ice Cream Man's body language was clear, he was making his move. Dan was mortified. He had no idea what to do, so he did nothing.

It went on for weeks this way, until suddenly, Dan saw something he simply could not abide. Ice Cream Man, who was a smoker, had just snuffed a cigarette out with his boot when he sauntered over to Lana like he had at least a dozen times. They talked for a minute, then Ice Cream Man reached for her.

Lana backed away, and Dan noticed a look of outrage on her face. Ice Cream Man was visibly upset. He stepped toward her again, this time grabbing her arm and pulling her close.

Even over the noise of traffic, Dan could hear Lana's scream. Without thinking, he charged across the intersection.

He dove to the left to dodge a honking BMW, and to the right to barely avoid a skidding VW bug. He stopped and took a step back, barely missing a speeding Toyota. He lifted his arms high as he leapt out of the path of an Escape.

His feathers flapped as he tumbled through the air to land on the nearby sidewalk.

Dan barreled into Ice Cream Man sending him flailing to the ground. Ice Cream Man careened across the sidewalk like a wayward barrel. Stunned and confused, Ice Cream Man helplessly wobbled about with his arms and legs in the air. Because of the bulkiness of his costume, he would need help getting up. Dan was not going to be the one to give it to him. Instead he turned to face Lady Lana Liberty for the very first time.

"Thank you," she said.

Dan just stood there.

"My name is Beatrice," she smiled.

"I'm Chicken Suit Larry," he said a little too loudly.

Buddy & Dean

Buddy lived on the side of a hill on the edge of a park. The park was not far from a liquor store where he would panhandle until he had enough money to buy a fifth of vodka. He would take it back the hill and drink until he passed out. It was his routine for 15 years.

15 years before, Buddy murdered a guy in self-defense. The act got under his skin. He started drinking to numb the pain and never stopped. The horrible memory of driving the knife into that man's gut was too overwhelming. The thought of it caused him to break down in sobs, as if it had happened just yesterday.

Buddy met Dean one day on the corner near the liquor store. Dean was a skinny dude with a long, scraggly beard and wild eyes. He held a cardboard sign that read: *Let's get real–I NEED BEER!!!*

Buddy was a burly man who had once been a boxer. To anyone on the street, it was clear who the alpha was. Buddy walked up on Dean with the intention of running him out of his territory. But when Buddy got close, Dean gave him a gap-toothed smile. He shook Buddy's hand and offered him a swig from his whiskey bottle. It was not the sort of thing that usually happened on the street. Buddy let it happen, because he was lonely. He couldn't remember the last time he had actually talked to anyone.

They had a great time together. Dean was the kind of guy who did whatever he could find: a little dope, a little blow, some ganja, a bit of crystal. He always seemed to have a little bit of everything. It was fun, but to Buddy the best part was having a friend in his life.

Dean was an emotional guy who had some serious highs and lows. Buddy's story touched him deeply. Maybe because it resembled his own. When Dean took a friend, he took him for life. The problem was Dean had never learned how to treat a friend. He would do everything to help Buddy, but when Buddy was laid out, Dean would not hesitate to take everything Buddy, had including clothes, bedding, and food. Buddy often woke up from his nightly stupor to discover everything he had was gone.

Dean had a knack for attracting trouble. When he drank, he acted crazy. The area police all knew him by name. Buddy tried to calm him down, but it never worked. One day, when Buddy refused to give him a dollar, Dean jabbed a pen knife into his arm. Buddy spilled blood all over the sidewalk. A passerby called 911. Buddy was taken to the hospital while Dean was taken to jail. Buddy swore if he ever saw Dean again, he would stick a knife in his gut, like the man he had killed so many years ago.

A few days later, in the hospital, Buddy was visited by a Homeless Outreach Worker; a lady named Rena. Something about the way she smiled made Buddy sign her papers. Before he knew it, he found himself in rehab. He spent 90 days sobering up, some of the best and worst days of his life. When he was done, Rena helped him get social security money and found him a studio apartment. There were many ups and downs on his road to a new life, but Buddy could not believe how quickly his life had changed.

One day, Rena came for her weekly visit. She had a somber look on her face. Buddy asked her what was the matter, thinking the worst. Maybe his past had come back to haunt him and he would be forced to go back onto the streets. If he had to, he knew he would have to kill himself first. There was no way he could go back to living on that hill.

"I thought you would want to know," Rena said tearfully. "Dean was found dead a few days ago. They think it was alcohol poisoning."

"Dean?" Buddy was shocked and confused. "But how do you know Dean?" he asked Rena. Buddy had not thought about his so-called friend for over six months.

"But didn't you know?" now she was surprised. "I met Dean in jail when he asked for help getting off the streets. He was the one who told me where to find you."

Buddy had no idea what to do other than weep.

The Story of a Rock

A rock sat alone on a hill. The hill was high and had a view of a beautiful grassy valley, but the rock was lonely.

Years went by, and the rock did not see a soul. Then, suddenly out of the blue, a bird landed on the rock. The rock tried to speak to it, but the bird was in a hurry and did not want to stop and chat. Many years later, a mouse scampered up the hill. The rock greeted it warmly, but it continued on its way down the other side. If the rock had eyes, he would have cried.

Five hundred years went by with the rock stuck on top of the hill. Until a tree sprouted up next to the rock. The rock was excited to have someone new to talk to, but the tree was too proud. It refused to even look at the rock because the rock was down in the dirt. The tree believed it was too good for something as filthy as a rock. It stuck to whispering to the wind.

Sadly the rock became bitter. He gave up on making friends. When a family of rabbits moved in, he did everything he could to run them off. He found that by shifting himself slightly in the earth he could make a loud thumping sound. Underground the thump was like a boom, so he thumped against the hill day and night until the rabbits were nearly driven mad. They ran down the hill to get away from the sound. If he wasn't so angry, the rock might have laughed.

Five hundred more years passed this way until something fortuitous happened. A crack of thunder filled the sky, and a heavy rain began to fall. The rain did not stop for many days, and as a result the hill turned to mud. The earth around the rock began to wash away, and the rock began to slide down the hill.

The rock had been on top of the hill for at least a thousand years, and for the first time he was moving. As quickly as the movement started, it was over. The rock plunged into a river at the bottom of the hill.

Five thousand years passed, and the rock had given up on the world. Occasionally, a school of fish would pause to nibble the algae off the rock. The rock would ignore them because he knew they would eventually swim away.

The rock would sometimes feel a rush of current that would lift him from the bottom of the river and carry him along for a short distance. Everything looked the same no matter where he was at the bottom of the river so the rock ignored this too.

One day, when he was tossed by the flowing water into a shallow pool, he could see the reflection of the surface on the top of the water and all the things that were happening in the world above. He grew to love the lush green of the plants and the dazzling blue of the sky and the puffy white of the clouds. Since he had something to enjoy, his heart grew a bit lighter.

Another ten thousand years passed, and a man was walking by the shore. He was staring into the water as if searching for something when he saw the rock. With a raise of his eyebrows, he reached into the pool and lifted the rock into the dry air.

"Perfect," the man said, and tossed the rock into a bag full of other rocks.

The man took the bag of rocks to his car where it rode for a very long distance. When the car finally stopped, the bag was brought into a house. The rock saw a whole family, including a dog and a cat. The rock was placed in a bowl where he was scrubbed and polished until he met with the man's approval.

The next day, the man took the rock into a garden where he spread concrete and very carefully placed the rock, and the other rocks, into a decorative pattern.

"Perfect," the man nodded when he was done, and walked into the house to clean himself.

"Hey," said another rock wedged in close to the rock. "Have I got a story for you." The rock would have smiled if he had a mouth.

"I can't wait to hear it," he answered. "And you won't believe the story I have for you."

As he listened to the other rock's story, for the first time he could remember, the rock did not felt alone.

Whiskers

People are very confusing. Some are very nice and some are not nice at all. Some smell better than others. Some are smarter than others. Strangest of all, they do not seem to speak a common language.

"Whiskers!" the big human will call in his booming voice.

"Whispers," the lady human will coo in her sweet voice.

"Whippers!" the little human will cry before smacking me with a book.

The day the little human came into my life has to be the worst of my life. From the beginning, he would grab my ears, my tail, my paws—whatever he could catch in his grubby little hands. I do my best to avoid him, but he always seems to find me. It's like he has a sixth sense. Maybe he can sense my fear.

Lately, I been scratching at the backdoor in the morning until the big human sets me free. I need this respite. I go to the bamboo forest behind the stone wall where I can sleep, undisturbed, in the shade. I chase down an occasional butterfly if I'm feeling hungry. But if I want real food, I have to saunter back into the house.

Sometimes I wonder what would happen if I walked beyond the bamboo forest. What would I see on the other side? Would there be other cats? Would they be friendly? Would we hunt and sleep together, and clean each others' fur? Or would they be mean and hiss at me, and try to scratch my eyes out?

It helps to think about all the good things in the people house, like the taste of wet meat on my tongue, my vast collection of rubber balls, the clump of fur I have hidden under the couch for a special occasion, my favorite sleeping spot near the heater, and the way the lady human strokes my fur and makes me purr like a kitten.

I guess things have changed for the better after the good thing I did for my people. A few days ago, the lady human fell asleep at her TV box while the little human was playing with blocks on the floor. Inevitably, he got bored and wandered off to cause trouble. Unfortunately, the lady human left the back door ajar when she brought me in for lunch. Of course, the little human went straight for it. His screaming woke me from my afternoon nap.

The lady human was sound asleep, so I ran out to see what was wrong. Somehow, the little human had gotten himself wedged into a small opening between the wall and the fence, the one I use to get to my bamboo forest. He was crying loudly and blood trickled down his face. I quickly bolted into the house and bounced off the lady human's face. She leapt into the air and nearly landed on her butt. I ran to the back door looking back at her and giving her my most obnoxious yowl.

"What's a matter with you?" she frowned, and that was when she heard the little one's cries. I have never seen her move so fast. She grabbed the little human, took him inside, and bandaged his head. And guess who got his own personal can of tuna that night.

There's a reason I'm here, I guess. Someone has to keep these people safe. I can't help wondering why the little human was heading to my bamboo forest. Could he have been just as curious as I am about what lies beyond?

The Old Coyote

I hear the people calling to me: "the Old Coyote!" I don't get mad. In a way, it makes me proud. Not many of us get to be old.

I know I'm near the end of my time, but I'm happy. I've done many good things, like the time my family was starving and I tracked the wounded deer. It was enough meat to last us through the winter. And the time I saved a brood of pups from a rabid badger. I still have the scars from that terrible fight.

My line will go on. I've had many children by many wives. Although I never see them, I know they're out there. I can hear them howling to me by the light of the full moon.

I left my family so that I wouldn't be a burden to them. It's the way of us. When one cannot keep up, it hurts everyone. The pack is only as strong as the weakest one. I could not be that one.

When I left, I roamed the people streets for a while. I dug in their garbage cans for food. I ate an occasional sick cat. But the people don't like these things. The people don't understand what it is to fight for survival. They took notice of me and even tried to kill me.

I ran away again, and traveled for many days and night. That's when I came to this place. It's a strange land. It looks half wild with wide open grass plains, but there are people places spread among the grounds. The people here are different than other people. They are old like me. When I first came, they left me bits of meat. It was welcomed, since I was close to death. When I felt better, I figured out how I could feed myself and be of use to the people here.

For some reason, the people like to cut the grass short. The gophers love this because they think it makes it easier for them to see us coming. In my many years, I have learned how to be a quiet and patient hunter. These gophers are fat and easy to catch. And they're everywhere! When I catch them, the people are very happy. The only thing gophers know how to do is dig, which ruins the grass. People dislike this more than they dislike me. Now they affectionately call me the Old Coyote.

The truth is, every day I grow more and more tired. It will not be long before I join the moon in the sky. I will see my mother again, and we will run together as we chase the stars. I've lived a good long life, and I deserve to run through the stars.

For the Birds

We keep close together. It fools the eyes of those who would devour us. Alone we are small and weak. Together we are many eyes, many voices, many wings.

Our song is deceptively simple, but very complex. Each of us has our own song that tells the history of our families. When we are together, we share our songs in a chorus of our legacy. This is the way we teach our children about our enemies, our failures, our successes. Sharing our song makes us stronger.

We hear the humans say, "For the birds". To them, it refers to something that is frivolous. It has a much deeper meaning for us. We say "for the birds" when we mean "for the good of all".

For the birds, we watch.

For the birds, we make song.

For the birds, we fly.

For the birds, we live.

And only then do we live.

The Ant

An ant tried to pick up a rock, but the rock was much too heavy for him.

"Help me move this rock," he said to another ant. It was a large rock by ant standards, and the queen had demanded that it be taken away from her kingdom because it was in her way.

Both ants tried to move the rock. One tugged, the other pushed. The rock did not move.

"It's too heavy," the second ant huffed. The first ant give him a look like, *well duh!*

"Go get more ants," the first ant sighed.

He waited for what seemed too long. Finally the second ant brought three more ants.

"What took you so long?" the first ant frowned.

"Everybody was busy," the second ant shrugged. His breath was sweet, and obviously, he had stopped for a sugar snack. The first ant was annoyed because he had not eaten all day.

"Okay everyone," the first ant called. "Let's all pull at the same time." The five ants pulled the rock at the same time. It did not move.

"Now try pushing it!" the first ant hollered. Still, the rock did not move.

"Rats," spat the first ant. The others gathered around waiting for him to come up with another idea.

"Bring all the ants you can find," the first ant said. "Bring the queen if you have to. It's going to take the entire colony to move this blasted rock." The other ants hesitated a moment before taking off in all different directions.

This time the other ants were gone for a very, very long time. The sun was starting to fall, and the first ant was extremely angry.

"Stupid ants," he cursed under his breath. "If I were the queen, things would be so different. The jobs would make sense. They would be jobs that any ant could do. For one thing, we wouldn't be wasting time trying to move ginormous rocks." That was when the entire ant colony arrived, including the queen.

"Tell us what to do," the second ant said.

The first ant stood on top of the rock so everyone could see and hear him.

"Now, everyone surround the rock!" he commanded. The other ants moved into place around the rock. The queen stood close by to watch, her hands on her hips.

"Now lift!" called the first ant.

All of the ants lifted at the same time. It was a serious struggle to get that thing off the ground. Every ant was wincing under the strain. They held it up, but could not move forward because of the weight of the giant rock. The queen was not pleased.

"What's wrong with you ants!" she screamed. "You can't even move a tiny, little rock? You're all useless! When I give an order, I want it followed! Move this rock now, you worthless bunch of lazy louts!"

In her fury, the queen ran under the rock. She used her big sharp pincers to prod and poke at the other ants. The ants made one final attempt to move, but of course, they could not. The queen kept snapping at them from her place under the rock. The rock suddenly slipped from their collective grasps and slammed to the ground.

The queen was gone.

For a moment, none of the ants moved.

Then, all the ants looked to the ant on top of the rock as if to say, *What do we do?* The first ant did not know what to do, so he did the only thing that he could think of.

"Everyone surround the rock!" he shouted.

Green

When I was little, my mother gave warnings in green, especially if there was something she did not want to do.

When I wanted to go swimming for the fifth day in a row and she did not want to take me, she said, "You're swimming too much. Your hair's going to turn green from all the chlorine."

Or, if there was something she wanted to stop me from eating, like white bread, she said, "Did you know that stuff turns green in your stomach?"

And when I was climbing a fence, or trying to get onto the roof, or digging my way under the house: "You're going to get a splinter in your leg and it's going to turn gangrene and the doctor will have to cut it off!"

Ironically green was her favorite color.

She covered herself in malachite jewelry with its multiple, swirling shades of green. She wore as much Kelly green clothing as she could get her hands on, and she put forest-green sheets on her bed. She even drove around in a bright, metallic green car. "The color is alien green!" she would announce proudly.

She was wrapped in a faded green blanket the day I watched her die.

Shortly before she passed, she told me, "Do the things you want to do. Live without regret." She lived by example, did the things she wanted to do, and died without regret.

So I opened up my computer, logged onto my blog and got ready to type another story.

I started with the title: *Green*

Animal Courage

"I won't let it happen again," the dog said with the kind of authority dogs liked to project when they were faced with injustice. The cat was dubious.

"What exactly do you think you can do about it?" she said through licks of her paw. As a cat should be, she was trying to be nonchalant, despite her worried stomach.

"Lots of things," the dog said, standing up to look more menacing. "My people are a proud race of warriors," he growled. "In the wilds, we made our own kills and—" He trailed off, trying to think of exactly what his people did in the wilds.

"Your people?" scoffed the cat. "You were born at the pet store. The only thing you ever killed was cans of Alpo and bags of Puppy Chow. You're no more a warrior than I am a fish."

The dog sat down with a defeated little whine.

"Well, we've got to do something," he said in a dejected tone.

The cat felt sorry for what she had said. They may not be the best of friends, but the dog was not her enemy either. They had grown up together, begrudgingly sharing the house with the lady whom they both adored unconditionally. While the dog was often annoying, especially when he was competing for the lady's affection, he could also be endearing. And while the cat mostly tolerated his presence, there were times she actually enjoyed having him around. Times like when he was protective against strangers. Or when he lay next to her on cold nights, when she allowed it. Or those rare moments when he shared some of his Alpo, which was really not that bad for dog food.

"You're right," the cat finally agreed. "We have to do something." If there was one thing they had in common, it was their absolute love for the lady.

"Let's sleep on it," she concluded. "We'll talk about it more in the morning." The cat decided that this night was cold enough for snuggling.

• • •

The lady had recently taken up with a gentleman who was anything but. He started out friendly enough, bringing gifts of flowers before dates at the opera or theatre. With his handsome face and charming voice, he swept the lady off of her feet, as they say.

The dog liked him immediately, as dogs are apt to do. The cat was more suspicious and kept her distance. But after a few weeks, even she could not deny his allure. First she rubbed his legs and mewed softly to which he responded by scratching her head. Several days later, she gingerly stepped onto his lap, and with soft purrs and movements of her paws, she signaled her acceptance.

Soon after that, the relationship got very serious. The man came around nearly every day. The lady hardly had time for herself, what with working all day and seeing the gentleman at night. It wasn't long before the gentleman was spending every weekend with her, and soon everything was far from perfect.

Following a particularly boisterous argument about where to go to eat one night, the gentleman slammed his fist into the wall leaving a large, round hole. He apologized over and over as he patched the wall with some plaster. The apology was taken, but the off-white patch remained like a scar. From that point on, the long weekends were often fraught with tension and outbursts.

Even worse, the cat could tell that the lady desperately desired time to herself. Only a cat, an animal that values alone time above all else, could sense such things. Despite the lady's attempts to be alone, the man continually insisted he be allowed to stay. He would tell her when he did not like the way she dressed, that he did not like the way she talked to other men. The lady, who was used to her independence, would laugh, which would make the man turn beet-red. At first, he held his anger inside. Until the day he snapped. The cat and the dog will never forget that day.

He turned his fury not against the wall, but onto the lady. He yelled at the top of his voice, "Stupid whore!" before picking up a small framed picture and lobbing it at her head. The lady ducked, and it smashed against the doorway. She quickly stepped behind the bedroom door, shutting and locking it. The door did not hold back the gentlemen's ire. He rammed into it with his shoulder, knocking it off its hinges. It collapsed with a boom, causing the dog to bark. "Shut the hell up!" the gentleman yelled as he kicked the dog hard, sending him yelping into the other room. He stomped into the bedroom and pushed the startled lady on the bed. He slapped her three times across the face. She didn't even have a chance to scream.

It was four weeks before the cat and the dog saw the gentleman again. In their minds, he had done the unthinkable and was no longer welcome in the lady's house. To their utter surprise, he walked in one day with a suitcase. Both he and the lady smiled and laughed as he swung her around and gave her a deep kiss. The cat could not help but notice the shiny rock ring on the lady's finger.

From that day, things only got worse. The beatings became more and more frequent, and more and more severe. The lady was bruised throughout her body, and she had a slight limp from a twisted ankle. Something was wrong with her arm, and it might even be broken. Both the dog and the cat could feel it; she was afraid for her life. And so were they.

∙ ∙ ∙

"We have to stop him in any way we can," the dog said when they woke up the one day.

The cat knew he was right, but she had no idea how they could possibly do so. The dog was big, at least a hundred pounds. The gentleman was more than twice that size. The dog had teeth, whereas the gentleman had two hands and his brains. In a fight, the gentleman held the clear advantage. Not to mention, the dog was afraid of the gentleman as he had suffered many beatings of his own.

The cat, who was better at avoiding the gentleman's rage, did not have the same fear, but she was at most five pounds. She had sharp claws, but what good were claws when she could easily be dispatched with a quick snap of the neck.

"Let's pee on his socks until he gets so grossed out he runs away," the dog said with a good-natured grin. He was a simpleton to be sure, but at least he was lovable.

"No," the cat said. "I have a better idea." She slowly licked her paw as she collected the specifics of her plan in her mind. "But we need to work together."

∙ ∙ ∙

It was set for the following Sunday, because the gentleman often spent Saturday nights drinking. After these binges, he was much more lethargic. The cat believed it would be easier to deal with him at this time.

The night before, it was impossible for either of them to sleep. They lay close together, each listening to the other's heartbeats, both dreading the day to come. They had no choice. The lady's life was at stake, and both of them would do anything they could to save her. Even lose their own lives.

• • •

That fateful Sunday, the cat awoke with a start. The day was further along than she had anticipated. Her plan was to get up before dawn to prepare, but it was now well past noon. Nearly in a panic, she charged toward the lady's room. She could hear the rhythmic snoring before she even got there. The gentleman was passed out in her bed. Then she heard a more ominous sound. She slowly followed it to the kitchen where she glimpsed a horrible sight. The lady was bent over the sink, blood dripping from her forehead. She clutched in her hands clumps of her long beautiful red hair. The top of her head was matted with bald red patches. What had that monster done to her…

Before the cat could rouse the dog, she heard the gentleman's ugly voice. He was getting up from the bed. The cat yowled in fear to which the gentleman responded by tossing a shoe. The cat shuffled away to find the dog. They had to act fast.

"Where are you bitch!" the man shouted in a groggy voice. The woman looked up from the sink, her eyes wide in terror.

"There you are," he said as he stepped into the kitchen. "Damn, you look horrible. How's about some eggs and bacon, bitch." She stood there staring at him, her breath pulsing in and out.

"What the hell's matter with you," he raised his voice. "Don't you fucking hear what I'm saying!?" He launched at her with fists raised.

Suddenly, the gentleman found himself flailing for air before landing on his face. The dog stood over him wagging his tail.

"Stupid dog tripped me!" he growled. Before he could stand, the dog sunk his teeth into the gentleman's shoulder.

"Fuck!" the gentleman yelled in surprise. The lady stepped back, her eyes unblinking.

The gentleman reached to grab the dog but was greeted by the claws of the cat. She wrapped her body around his hand and dug in deep.

"Ahhhh!" the gentleman screamed. He shook his hand and tried to kick at the dog, but both animals were in a frenzy.

"Help me!" he yelled at the lady. His yell snapped her out of her trance. She looked around her. Without thinking, she picked up a large clay pot from the floor. She hefted it over her head.

"What are you—" The gentleman never finished his sentence. The pot came down hard, smashing to pieces over his head. His death was almost instantaneous.

• • •

The trials were long, and the woman attended a year of therapy to deal with what the gentleman had done to her mind and body. Eventually, she was acquitted for self-defense. Eventually she was able to move on with her life. As always, the cat and the dog stayed close by her side, every step of the way.

Death's Dilemma

Death had a sister named Rose who thought his job was stupid, and took every opportunity to tell him so.

"Only a loser would get off on killing people," she often said.

"I'm not killing people," Death always countered. "And I don't get off on it."

Death use to get mad at her for saying these things until he realized that she did it because she was unhappy with her own life. Somehow, it made her feel better about herself to put him down.

One day, the worst imaginable thing happened. Death was given Rose as his next victim.

Death thought a long time about their years growing up together. Rose was older and had always been mean to him. She teased him, hit him, and called him names. But none of this was any reason to want her to die.

Of course, it was not his job to decide who would die. He was only the messenger, and once he was given a victim there was no questioning it. It was after all his job.

He tried to draw it out by avoiding her, but she was the kind of person who would push herself on someone if she felt like they were trying to stay away from her.

She called him several times a day. Each day, the messages got meaner and meaner. She belittle him constantly. She started bring up things from his childhood, things that really hurt him. Like the time his prom date canceled at the last minute. Or the time a kid punched him in the stomach and stole his shoes. Or the time his class gave him the nickname Boney, which had pretty much stuck throughout his school years.

Death started to think maybe it wouldn't be so bad if she were gone. His whole life, all she had ever done was terrorize him and make him feel like nothing. If she only knew what he had to do to her. How would she treat him then?

The day came when he could no longer put it off. So he sadly walked the distance to her apartment, opened her front door, and stepped inside to greet her.

"Why are you wearing your stupid death robe?" were her last words.

When she was gone, he could not feel anything. His only thought, as he looked down on her body, was how peaceful she looked. He had never seen her look so peaceful and quiet. It wasn't such a bad thing, seeing her that way.

The Backyard War

Robby nooked a pebble into the pocket of his slingshot. He stretched back the band as far as he could. The pocket slipped from his eleven year old hand, and the stone fell in front of him with a useless thud.

"Aw man," he lamented.

"Lemme try!" cried Becka, his six year old sister.

"No, Becka," Robby chastised. "Only for big kids."

"I'm big," Becka pouted with arms crossed before giving up to find something else to do.

Robby picked up the rock and tried again. This time he was able to keep the band steady and fire it off a few yards. Better, but not quite good enough. He needed more practice.

"My turn," Becka, who had come back for another try, whined.

"No, Becka," Robby said firmly. "This is serious business. Now let me concentrate." He felt bad for being mean to his sister, but this really was very serious business.

It started out innocently enough. Magpies had been Robby's favorite bird for as long as he could remember. He loved the startling black and white feathers with the shock of blue in the wing. He admired their high pitched calls and their bright and curious eyes. There was one bird in particular that Robby adored, a magpie he called Alexander.

One day Robby left some bits of watermelon in a bowl in the yard, and Alexander consumed them with great relish. After that day, he began to follow Robby around the yard. Robby started feeding him daily, and a few days later, Alexander brought a gift. It was an old copper penny dated 1942 with wheat stalks on one side. It was like no other penny Robby had ever seen.

"That's not something you see every day," his mom said. "Keep it and it may be worth something in the future."

As the days passed, Alexander brought many things: a cracked watch face, a piece of a Dayglo frisbee, a McDonald's french fry box, a green golf ball, a page from a book about mermaids, the arm of a Ninja Turtle action figure, an empty travel-size Crest toothpaste tube, a bent, silver hoop earring, a dozen buttons in all shapes, sizes and colors, countless bottle caps, a small, broken, combination lock, a large, glass marble, a tangled gold chain, assorted feathers of all types, a bit of copper wire, the blade-less hilt of a kitchen knife, a plastic fishing lure shaped like a minnow, a pink baby spoon, a rusty nail, a bleached out photograph, a mysterious electrical component, a tarnished brass key, half of a five dollar bill, a torn, miniature American flag, a coupon for Round Table pizza, a hollowed out writing pen, a pencil without an eraser, and a Jack of spades playing card.

Robby and Becka were enchanted by the offerings. Every morning, they woke up early to see what Alexander left on the doorstep. Sometimes, Alexander perched in a nearby tree, as if he wanted to see the children's reactions.

The family became so enamored with Alexander's shenanigans that they began to coax him inside the house. Robby's mom left the kitchen window open and a plate of goodies on the table. She put out his favorites of soggy bread, peeled grapes, pine nuts, dried cranberries, and, of course, diced watermelon.

Alexander eyed the booty from the safety of his nearby tree. Eventually, he felt brave enough to hop onto the windowsill for a few seconds before taking off into the garden. It took several more days for Alexander to overcome his shyness and take the leap through the window onto the kitchen table. He fluttered into the room, took half a grape, and darted back out the window. Not long after that, Alexander was comfortable enough to explore.

He focused on the kitchen first. For a long time, he stared at his reflection in a copper pot. Another time, he sputtered about in the soapy water in the sink. Some utensils jangled under his feet which sent him scurrying for the window.

The living room was Alexander's next stop where he was fascinated, yet fearful, of the tiny people in the large, black square hanging on the wall. He would cock his head sideways to glare at them with one eye, then turn his head to peek with his other eye. He never got used to the squawk box, and generally avoided it by passing quickly through the dining room to get to the upstairs.

Upstairs, Alexander found an endless collection of wonders. In a hallway mirror, he admired himself from the tip of his beak to the end of his tail. In Robby's bedroom, he found an electronic keyboard. Alexander walked up and down on the keys creating cacophonous music to which he added an occasional trill.

In Robby's mother's room, he discovered a veritable treasure trove. It was a small box of costume jewelry. From that day forward, each day, he took one shiny piece of plastic jewelry and brought it to wherever magpies keep their personal riches. Because it was old costume jewelry, Robby's mother did not mind. In fact it was a bit of a relief to get rid of some junk she had no intention of using.

Things went on this way happily and harmlessly for some time until one morning when Robby and Becka awoke to their mother's panicked screaming: "No! No! No!"

Robby ran to his mother's room to find her sobbing on the edge of her bed. He walked over to comfort her, and when she looked at him, all she could say was, "His ring…"

Not quite a year ago, Robby's father died. He was in excellent health, physically fit from a rigorous daily exercise routine that included nightly runs. Sadly there was a defect in his heart that had never been detected, and one night, after a particularly grueling jog, he collapsed a few feet from the doorstep. The sudden, inexplicable loss left a hole in the family, a hole that Alexander seemed to fill.

It was part of Robby's mother's daily ritual to hold and look at her husband's wedding ring. It was one of her only remaining connections to her lost love. This morning, the ring was not in its usual place. It was nowhere to be found.

There was only one possible suspect—Alexander the magpie. After all the kindness they had shown him, how could Alexander do this to his mother? Besides the death of his father, it was the worst betrayal of Robby's young life. In the midst of his grief, all Robby could think about was revenge. Thus, he found himself sitting in the garden with slingshot in hand awaiting the magpie's inevitable return.

Becka got bored again, leaving Robby alone with his thoughts. Unexpectedly, he found himself crying. It was the first time since his father's death he had been able to cry, and it made him feel even angrier.

In the stillness that followed, Robby heard a familiar sound, "Wock wock-a-wock wock!" In the past, the sound would have elicited a feeling of joy. The magpie had become his best friend in a time of need. Now, with the seriousness of his crime, Alexander had become Robby's worst enemy.

There was a flash of black and white near the plum tree, Alexander's favorite place to perch. Reflexively Robby pulled back the band and shuffled through the grass. As he approached the tree, Alexander gave a whistle and drifted above Robby's head. It was their custom, a kind of greeting. Robby was counting on it. He took a moment to aim before letting the first pebble fly. There was a cry of pain and fright as Alexander fell to the ground. As he stumbled about, it was clear his wing was broken. Dazed, he lay in the grass attempting to get his bearings. This was his undoing. Robby loomed over him. He leveled another shot and sent it straight to the bird's head. Alexander's death was instant.

Robby stood over the lifeless body, his thoughts swirling in a haze. It happened so quickly, so easily. For a moment, he was not quite sure what he had done. Then, through his mind's fog, he heard a voice. His mother was calling to him. Robby did his best to focus on what she was saying. In order to understand her, he had to look away from the mess in front of him.

"I found it!" she shouted from her bedroom window. "It fell behind the bed! It was there the whole time!"

Living In a Truck

Scoot lived in an old, red GMC pickup truck. He was sixty-seven years old, without a penny to his name. He couldn't get a job if he wanted to, even though he could fix just about anything that wasn't a computer.

Scoot dropped out of high school and never looked back. He didn't see the wisdom in school. It was easier to work and make money. He decided to never marry after a girl broke his heart when he was 23. "You don't got no ambition," she told him when he asked her to marry him.

Scoot got his name because he use to collect and fix old motor scooters. He had a garage full of parts. People from all around would come to have him fix their scooters. He made a modest living at it, but was never really able to save anything. Sadly, he never bothered to study up on the parts he acquired. Turns out, one time he had a rare Vespa worth 10,000 dollars. A dishonest picker convinced him to sell it for 500 measly dollars.

After he retired, Scoot had nothing but his big red truck. So he took to the road, and whenever he found something worth keeping, he tossed it into the back of his truck. Bicycles, strollers, shopping carts, whatever he could fit. Whenever he found someone who needed something, he'd dig in the back of his truck, and nine times out of ten, he found what they wanted. The people in town were so poor that he rarely charged them for it.

Scoot was a big guy. Living in a truck took its toll on his body. One harsh Winter came, and he barely lived through it. Summers he chose to sleep outside on the ground. Then one day, when he was buying some Doritos and a Coke at 7-Eleven, he came back to find his truck was gone.

Scoot felt like laying down to die. All his life he had done nothing but give to other people, and this was the thanks he got. What could he do but give up.

When the people in town found out, they rallied around him. They found him a place to live. They gave him food to eat, and whatever else he needed.

Scoot was an unhealthy man, so he did not live much longer after that, but he lived the rest of his life surrounded by people who cared.

Life at the Lake

Life at the lake was pretty great until the worst happened.

Oh, we had our difficulties. Nothing is perfect. It was never a picnic when the geese came. They flew in by the hundreds, the nasty bastards! They thoroughly enjoyed chasing us off the shore with their obnoxious hissing. They ate everything in sight. It's asinine behavior, I'll agree, but hardly anything to get your feathers in a twist over.

Needless to say, we ducks are much more civilized. We exist within a strict hierarchy where status is determined by who is the largest. The bigger the duck, the more he matters.

The biggest duck at the lake was named Joey. He's a pretty decent bird, all things considered. He's got this booming quack that you can hear all the way across the water. When Joey quacks, everybody comes running, flapping, swimming, whatever. He happens to be the best at finding algae beds where minnows and tadpoles like to hide.

One time Joey quacked across the lake, and we all came rushing over to find a very bizarre sight. These big, pink, featherless ducks were throwing food into the water. You might ask how I know these things are ducks. It's simple, really. If you quack at them, they will quack back.

These ducks don't always make sense in their responses. Once I quacked: "How do you do?" to which one of them quacked back: "Why yes, the clouds are quite fishy today!" The real mystery is how they lost feathers.

Last Winter, the freaky, pink ducks did something terrible to us. Maybe they were upset about having to share the lake with us. They never seem to go into the water, so I'm not sure why they would be so territorial. Maybe they were mad because they thought we wouldn't share food with them, which is not true. Joey quacks to them the same way he quacks to us whenever he finds something good to eat. Probably, they were jealous of our feathers.

Anyway, a group of them trapped a bunch of us in nets. They pulled us to shore where they strangled our necks and threw our dead bodies in bags. They did not take all of us. Thankfully, I was one of the ones who escaped.

Watching my friends die gave me nightmares for weeks. I don't think I will ever completely get over what those pink ducks did to us. What saved me was that my best friend, Leonard, figured out a plan. We recruited Joey to help us convince others to join. The next time a group of pink weirdos came to feed us, we ignored the food and attacked them. We bit them with our beaks. We scratched them with our feet. We slapped them with our wings.

Damn, if we didn't send those pink freakazoids scrambling back across the grass. It felt great. We were taking back what was ours.

That was when the geese returned. Since they are big and stubborn, they refused to believe us when we told them about the murderous pink ducks. We watched in dismay as the geese greedily gobbled up their offerings. Inevitably, the nets were turned onto the geese.

"We warned you!" we said as they honked in fear and dismay. When it was over, the geese that remained were more than willing to join our cause.

If you think we were formidable as a gang of ducks, imagine what we were with a gaggle of angry geese in tow. I'll give those guys one thing, they know how to fight! Together we were able to chase those stupid pink ducks off for good.

Now we follow the geese. It turns out, they know where a lot of other great lakes are. And as long as we are banded together against the horrible pinks, we have nothing to worry about. Sure we have to put up with the geese, but all things considered it could be a lot worse.

Freedom of Imagination

I

Margaret liked to watch the squirrels in the courtyard from the window by her bed. She even gave them names: Scrunch, for the one that always crouched down in the grass; Wobbles, for the one that drank fermented nectar from the camellias which made him stumble like a drunk; Bloaty, for the one that was almost twice as big as the others; and Tater, for the one that sat around all day on the fence like a little couch potato. She spent a lot of time thinking up adventures for them. She imagined the squirrels practicing harmonies of Cole Porter songs as they taught the mourning doves and house finches to dance like a miniature chorus line. She giggled at the thought of them dressed in tiny slacks, pressed shirts, mini bowties, and bowler hats before standing beneath the tall oak trees where they would call on their respective girlfriends who were done up in fancy flared skirts and low cut blouses. She wondered what would happen if they somehow got into a car and found the keys, and turned the ignition and drove themselves around Tijuana to drink the night away on tequila and Coronas before ambling home sick the next day. It was a silly diversion, but a welcomed way to while away the endless hours.

Margaret was always told she had quite an imagination. When she was younger, the nuns at elementary school frowned upon what they deemed her "overactive" imagination and "day-dreamy" nature. Her father noticed, with great frustration, her penchant for things like story writing and drawing. He called her imagination "troubling," and worked to steer her toward more practical pursuits, like accounting, nursing, and computer programming. None of these interested Margaret in the least.

She dreamed of being an animator, of making funny and sad cartoons with silly, but lovable, characters. She dreamed of drawing little animals and putting them in goofy adventures on the big screen, much like her courtyard squirrels. But lately, whenever she attempted to put pencil to paper, she froze. She could not get her hand to move. She could not express on paper the things that were going on in her mind.

Margaret was in graduate school for marine biology, something she settled into for her father's sake. She was failing her classes, which sent her into a downward spiral of anxiety and depression. This plunge into darkness eventually lead her to standing on the rooftop of her fourteen story dorm building. The whole fiasco cost her university about $10,000 in emergency fees when the fire department, police, and ambulance were brought to the scene. The result was a 72-hour hold in a psychiatric hospital for danger to self, which then lead to a 14-day hold for medication stabilization.

By day 5, Margaret had given the squirrels their names and backstories.

On day 7, her father came to visit all the way from San Francisco. The look on his face brought tears to her eyes. She could not tell if he was concerned about her, or disappointed in her. When she suddenly realized that she pretty much always believed he was disappointed in her, she could not continue the visit.

Day 9 was her best day since being admitted. She met another patient she felt she could talk to, another college girl named Millie. They hit it off immediately, and Margaret introduced Millie to her squirrel friends. Tater was Millie's favorite because she could relate to his sedentary nature. Millie was good at telling jokes, and for the first time in as long as she could remember, Margaret found herself laughing.

Day 10, Margaret's mother came to see her, and Margaret sat there holding her as she cried. Her mother kept blaming herself, saying over and over again it was her fault. Margaret insisted several times that it was not. As always with her mother, Margaret found herself acting as the parent.

Day 12, Margaret answered the psychiatrist's inquiry differently for the first time. Instead of saying her usual "Fine" when he asked how she was doing, she said, "I feel like things are getting clearer." The psychiatrist nodded approvingly and stated, "The medications are working."

Day 13, she was feeling bored. She brought out her sketch pad and started doodling. She drew her four squirrels all in a row with cheesy smiles on their faces.

Day 14, Margaret was released on schedule. She said goodbye to all the nurses whom she knew by name, to the doctor, to the staff, to Millie, who exchanged numbers with her, and to the squirrels. Her plan was to leave grad school and to go back home where she would meet with a therapist once a week. From there, she did not really know what she would do next. The not knowing gave her, for the first time in her life, a true sense of freedom.

II

*Imagination is the only weapon
in the war against reality!*

This was the tattoo on her back. This was what drew Mike to her. It set his own imagination reeling. What was this mysterious lady all about? Was she a starving artist who constructed giant mosaics of painted rocks and broken tiles? Was she a pothead inclined to catchy clichés and crazy cat memes? Was she secretly a private detective searching for a maniacal serial killer? Or was she some kind of crazed killer out for innocent blood?

Mike had a very spry imagination, and in the thirty seconds following his sighting of this strange woman, he manufactured in his mind several possible first-date scenarios. The first included a midnight boat ride over calm, glowing, purple waters above a dancing full moon; the second, a long night of dancing dressed in evening finery, concluded with cocktail at a swanky, dive-y nightspot (Manhattan for him, Cosmopolitan for the lady); and the third, a local coffee shop for deep conversation and a poetry open-mic where he would dazzle her with his amateurish, yet passionate verses.

Mike was forced to snap awake from his daydreaming when the woman finished paying the gas station attendant and turned toward the glass door.

"Nice tattoo," he said shyly.

"Oh," the woman replied nervously. "Thanks."

He immediately regretted speaking to her. The illusion of mystery was utterly destroy by the awkwardness that floated between them. She continued on her way, and in an instant, she was gone.

III

Margaret eventually went to school for animation. Sadly, her father disowned her because of this, which ultimately caused her mother to leave him. Her mother also went back to school. She wanted to become a nurse. She was also Margaret's biggest cheerleader, calling her at least once a week to check in on her progress.

Margaret was so adept at making up stories and characters, that she quickly rose through the ranks. As a producer, she made quite a bit of money on a cartoon series entitled *The Squirrely Bunch*. It was hard to believe that she was actually doing the thing she loved most. When she found herself with downtime between projects, she decided to do something to give back. The library was one of her favorite places, and it was a place desperate for volunteers.

Her first day was spent alone in the basement, filing phone books from other countries. It was tedious and lonely, but she told herself she was helping, even if it felt like she was not. It went on like this for a few months. Margaret considered complaining or quitting. In the end, both ideas seemed ridiculous. Someone needed to file those phone books. Why shouldn't it be her?

Eventually, the library staff trusted her enough to allow her to shelve books in the stacks. The work was much more interesting, primarily because she was able to interact with other people, some of which included the local homeless population who used the library for shelter in the day time.

IV

Herman had a neatly trimmed beard and flowing white hair that he kept hidden in a ponytail. He liked to brag that he had not cut his hair in five years, but the truth was that it was another expense he could not afford. Herman lived out of his truck because he did not have enough money to pay rent. He got about 650 dollars a month from social security. It was enough for a couple of meals a day at Del Taco or McDonald's, and a monthly membership at YMCA where he could clean himself up a few times a week.

Herman carried his life in a Swiss Army backpack: a first-generation iPad that his brother gave him, which he used to watch old shows and movies on Netflix, a fancy, ivory-handled shaving kit that he inherited from his father, a Zippo lighter decorated with an etching of the Beatles, a pocket knife with over 80 different features, a rusty 8" inch crescent wrench left over from his working days, a small hunk of golden quartz he found on a desert trip many years ago, his three favorite books (*The Sun Also Rises*, *Catcher in the Rye*, and *Watership Down*), a few assorted notebooks filled with lines of poetry and some short stories, and a small broken revolver.

Herman's truck had a camper shell which housed a full-size mattress where he slept at night with his grey tabby cat Mitzi. Mitzi was getting on in years, so she no longer had the urge to stray. She spent her days snoozing on the mattress. Herman made sure her food and water bowls were full and her small litter box was clean. Other than some pillows and blankets, there was no room for much more. If he needed to spend a day or two indoors, Herman might splurge for a motel near the end of the month. If money was tight, he might show up at his nephew's apartment where he was always welcome to sleep on the couch for a night or two.

Herman whiled away the days in the local library, where Margaret was a volunteer. One day, Margaret noticed that Herman was reading East of Eden, her favorite book. Soon she found herself wrapped up in a conversation that started with the theme of timshel, or free will, went on to questioning what true freedom means, and ended with questions about Margaret herself. She told Herman that she was an animator, to which Herman's eyes lit up.

"Curious coincidences," he smiled. "My nephew is obsessed with animation. You two should meet." Margaret laughed in response and quickly got back to work.

But Margaret could not stay away from this intriguing, older man who held such wisdom. She would take her breaks in the library coffee shop with him where they would discuss his latest read. It was like their own private book club. Herman was sensitive enough to know not to bring up his nephew again. Truthfully, he was just happy to have some pleasant, thoughtful company.

"Don't take your freedom for granted," he said pointedly one day when they were discussing the book *Fahrenheit 451*. Considering her past, Margaret thought these were the truest words ever spoken.

V

Herman did not show up to the library for a few days. It did not worry Margaret at first, as he was sometimes known to miss a few days here and there. But then, a few days turned into a few weeks, a few weeks into a few months. Margaret feared the worst. She knew so little about him. He was secretive and avoided personal questions. Any time she tried to offer him money, he would politely refuse. After a few times, she stopped offering because she could almost feel the pained expression on his face.

What could I have helped him with? the thought ran endlessly in her mind. *Find him a place to live? Find him a counselor to talk to?*

Just when Margaret felt like she might lose her mind with worry, a man about her age approached her holding a few worn books.

Probably going to ask me to shelve them, she thought, so she started to tell him where the book drop was.

Before she could say a word, he said, "Margaret?"

She nearly jumped back and ran.

"I'm Herman's nephew," he said nervously. "I don't mean to bother you but he really wanted you to have these after he… passed away."

He held up a tattered little stack of books. She slowly took them from him, unsure of what to say. She opened the first one, *The Sun Also Rises*, and read an inscription:

> *Dear Margaret,*
> *Thank you for your kindness to*

> *an old man. It's interactions like the ones we had that truly make us free.*
>
> *Herman*

She had never read any of these books before. She held them close as tears suddenly formed in her eyes.

"Hey," the man said as he reached for her, then stopping himself. "You did so much for him, I hope you know," he said. "He always talked about you and all the great talks you had. Thank you for being willing to listen." The man turned to leave.

"Wait," Margaret said. "What is it about these books… ?" She did not quite know how to phrase her question. The man frowned a little, as if he were thinking of how to begin.

"Well, when he talked about them with me, my uncle always said they were different illustrations of the costs of freedom. They teach us how to be grateful for it and not take it for granted."

Considering all she had been through in the past, these words forced a sob from Margaret's throat. She involuntarily dropped the books to the floor.

When Mike moved to help her pick them up, he was startled to see something familiar. Margaret had gotten it shortly after she left the psychiatric hospital many years ago. It was a tattoo on her back that read:

> *Imagination is the only weapon in the war against reality!*

Hilde

As Giselle sat to rest in the shade of a sprawling oak tree, she heard the familiar, soft *chuk-chuk* sound coming from her backpack. She quickly pulled it open to see if Hilde was okay. Downy brown tail feathers appeared first. Giselle carefully reached in and lifted the small chicken into the open air. Hilde flicked her tiny head from side to side, peering at Giselle. That look usually made Giselle smile, but not this time.

Night was falling, and Giselle had no idea where she was going. In her eleven years, Giselle had been very few places: the house and her father's farm, of course; the general store with her mother; the feed store with her father; the local schoolhouse; Ms. Avery's, when there was no one else to watch her; assorted relatives; and a time or two in a nearby city she could never remember the name of. Unfortunately, she could go to none of these places.

Giselle sat in the grass as Hilde scratched at a patch of dirt. She watched, entranced, as Hilde eyed a spot intently then snatched up a slimy earthworm. Hilde swallowed it like a long piece of spaghetti and fluffed her feathers as if she were proud of herself. Giselle was finally able to smile.

To be a chicken, she thought wistfully. Away from the farm, Hilde didn't have a care in the world. She had no idea what was waiting for her there. Giselle refused to think about it.

"That's why we left," she said out loud. Giselle dug into her backpack and found a bag of Cheez-its. She popped a few into her mouth and tossed some to Hilde, who eagerly pecked them to pieces.

A tear came to Giselle's eye as she watched the little chicken work at the bright orange crackers. Why did her father have to be so mean?

"Life on the farm," he always said. It was his excuse for butchering piglets and calves into cutlets, roasts and sausages. How many times had Giselle sat crying at the dinner table for the loss of another friend. Yes, friends was what she considered them. What else would they be? She lived on a farm, far away from other children. She had no brothers or sisters. The animals were her only friends.

Boris the hog, who liked to gnaw on corn cobs and tickled Giselle's face with the bristles on his snout, was turned into Sunday dinner for Reverend Balstein and his fat wife who both smacked their lips and gushed at the meatiness of the pork tenderloin. "I had six servings!" the Reverend bragged as he patted his bulging belly. Ilka the German shepherd, who liked to chase squirrels and dig up gophers as well as sleep curled up with Giselle under the warm down blanket at night, was "put out of her misery" when she came home one day whining and limping. "Can't have a lame farm dog," her father gave that familiar scowl. Dieter the ram, who willingly allowed her to snuggle up to his soft, woolly coat if she fed him carrots and apples, was barbecued whole for a community feast for people from miles around, most notably a gang of brats that teased Giselle for her worn overalls and plaid shirt. It was then Giselle decided that she did not like farm children and avoided contact with them at all costs. Animals were better than people anyway. And then there was Hilde.

Hilde was unremarkable by chicken standards, scrawny most would say. To Giselle's father, she was a nuisance. She would not lay eggs, and therefore she was best served baked, stewed, or fried. To Giselle, Hilde was a best friend. She followed Giselle around the house and yard as she did her chores. She shared meals with Giselle, because chickens can eat just about anything. She nestled in Giselle's bed at night next to her feet. She woke Giselle up in the morning with her soft *chuk-chuk*. So the day her father decided that Hilde would be dinner was the day Giselle decided to run away.

"Nobody's going to kill you, Hilde," Giselle said wiping away another tear. Giselle made ready to leave when a loud, crunching sound filled the glade. A frightened Hilde fluttered into Giselle's lap. Giselle's heart pounded as a tall, black shadow stepped out from behind a tree. A flashlight beam blinded Giselle and sent Hilde sputtering in a stand of bushes.

"Hilde, no!" Giselle called.

"Giselle?" said a shaky voice. It was her father.

"Go away!" Giselle shouted. She instinctively grabbed at whatever she could find and threw it toward the towering figure: handfuls of grass, small sticks, a few pebbles.

"Leave us alone!" she yelled in a tone she did not know she possessed.

"Giselle," her father said sadly, dodging her projectiles.

"You can't kill her," she said, her voice breaking. "You can't kill my friends!" She crawled into the nearby bushes in which Hilde had disappeared.

"Giselle, wait—" there was desperation in her father's voice. The flashlight beam skipped about frantically.

Pushing through the bushes was like navigating a jungle at midnight. As Giselle forced her way through the tangle of branches, she could feel them ripping cuts and gashes into her skin. She didn't care. She had to find Hilde and get away.

"Giselle..." her father pleaded. He had not yet followed her. Maybe he was too large to squeeze in the bushes.

"Hilde?" Giselle said, barely above a whisper. She stopped to listen. She knew there was no way she could find the chicken by sight in the blackness, but if she could hear her *chuk-chuk*, maybe she could locate Hilde. With a thick web of bramble above her, Giselle kneeled down to listen. Her father was quiet for the moment.

Many sounds greeted Giselle in the night. She did her best to interpret them: the frantic, cacophonous chirp of a thousand crickets; the faraway bark of a forlorn hound dog; an occasional high-pitched screech that may or may not have been a barn owl; an unidentifiable, metallic ring that made her a bit nervous. Then she heard it. 'Chuk-chuk chuk-chuk chuk-chuk.'

"Hilde!" she said with relief. The chicken was within arm's reach. Giselle reached out to stroke her soft feathers. Her touch calmed the bird. She came closer until she was underneath Giselle. Giselle was able to maneuver her backpack off of her shoulder and gently pushed the chicken inside.

Giselle was exhausted by her efforts. She set the bag beside her, trying to figure out what to do next. Her body and mind only wanted rest. The leaves beneath her were so comfortable. Soon, she could not help but fall asleep.

• • •

Giselle awoke to the chirping of a hundred songbirds. The sunlight blazed its way through the mess of branches above her. For a few moments, she thought she was at home in bed where she must've left the window open. Her first thought was to get up and close the shade so that she could go back to sleep. Her second thought was about the night before.

"Hilde," she thought. She clutched the bag close and slowly unzipped it. Hilde's shiny black eyes meet hers, and Giselle could not help but giggle.

"Good morning, girl," she said as Hilde began scratching the ground for her breakfast. Giselle's tummy rumbled at the thought of food, but she had nothing left to eat. As she considered how to go about getting breakfast, the bushes above her parted and her father's face appeared. In the night, he went back to the farm to get a machete to clear away the bracken. He was too afraid to chop at the bushes in the dark. He feared he might harm Giselle. Instead he spent all night, wide awake, desperately waiting for morning and the chance to find her. As soon as dawn came, he cleared a path to her.

"Please," Giselle begged as she burst into tears. "Please don't." There was none of the usual anger in her father's face. It was only concern. He could not seem to look her in the eye.

"I'm not gonna kill 'er," he simply said. "Now let's go home."

A huge wash of relief consumed Giselle. She had done the right thing. Her father finally understood. Hilde was going to live.

But where was Hilde?

Her father chopped and chopped through the sea of twisted briar, but Hilde could not be found. Giselle was sobbing when her father told her that they must give up and go home. They started to leave when Giselle noticed it sitting in a shallow divot not far from where she lost Hilde. One tiny, green egg was waiting for her.

The Christmas Spam

Ben lost his job shortly before Christmas. "The work's dryin' up," his boss told him, sadly.

Ben hauled for a small lumber company that was hit hard by the construction lull. He knew this day was coming, but he never thought it would happen around Christmas.

"But it's Christmas," he nearly pleaded.

"Which is worst time of year for this work, what with the snow and all," his boss shook his head. "Sorry, Ben."

So it was on Christmas Eve Ben found himself with no money for his family's holiday. He hadn't told his wife and kids. He didn't know how to tell them. As with every year, they were expecting the works: Christmas tree, presents, turkey dinner.

As everyone slept, Ben shuffled aimlessly through the house not knowing what to do. He looked through the garage and the closets as if they might hold some secret answer. He ended up in the kitchen where he could only find his wife's stockpile of Spam. There were dozens and dozens of shiny, blue cans lining the shelves. Ben plucked a few of them off the shelf and placed them on the kitchen table.

"Who in the world buys so much Spam?" he shook his head.

Disturbed out of his slumber, the dog looked over to see Ben folded over the kitchen table weeping in his arms.

Then, suddenly, a desperate idea occurred to Ben. He stood up and began pulling every last can of Spam from the shelf. He laid down a plastic table cover and popped open each can of Spam, dumping the slimy, pink bricks onto the table. When he had a substantial pile, he grabbed a butter knife and began to work.

The first thing he made out of Spam was an X-box, complete with two controllers and several games. It was exactly what his two boys wanted. Next, he formed a Barbie doll with a Barbie Corvette, his little girl's desired gift. He sculpted a small Spam Christmas tree with tiny Spam ornaments. Lastly he constructed a turkey feast with all the trimming, entirely from Spam. When he was done at around four o'clock in the morning, he looked over what he had created.

"Not bad," he smiled in a half daze. "Maybe they won't know the difference." As he was dozing at the table, he thought of one more gift. Carefully he crafted a small diamond ring for his wife, the one gift he had never been able to afford for her. As he drifted off to sleep, he thought how happy she would be to have it. "If only it was real…" he mumbled in a half-dream.

"Dad!" a noise came from the darkness. "Dad! Dad!"

Ben startled awake to see his youngest son, Eddie's face close to his.

"This is the best Christmas ever!" he cried before running back to join his brother to play Fallout on their new X-box.

"Daddy, I love my doll!" said his daughter as she kissed him on his cheek. He hugged her, enjoying the feel of her warmth against his body. That was when he noticed his wife sitting across from him with tears streaming down her cheeks.

"It's beautiful," she whispered. Ben saw the large diamond gleaming on her finger. She got up to give him a passionate kiss. Everything was exactly as he hoped it would be.

"And if it's a dream," Ben thought. "I never want to wake up."

Martin Luthers

"Luther's a weird name," said a skinny, bald guy with liver spots on top of his head.

"Be nice, Martin," said a woman whose boobs were bigger than the bald guy's head. Back in the day, Luther would have enjoyed such things, but the way these sagged made his stomach turn, not to mention that his old willy couldn't do anything, even if he wanted.

"What nice," Martin scoffed. "Alls I said is, it's a weird name."

"Put both your names together, and you become a 60s civil rights leader," said a second woman with a sharp nose and thick glasses. "Better than the sum of your parts for sure," she laughed.

"A what now?" Martin gave a confused look.

"She means Martin Luther King," the boobs lady said apologetically. "You know. I have a dream." She smiled good-naturedly which annoyed Luther even more. All of the people here annoyed him. They were old, which reminded him that he was old.

"He wasn't the first Martin Luther," Luther grumbled.

"I beg your pardon?" said the boobs lady.

"He's referring to Martin Luther of Protestant Reformation fame," answered the smart lady who was clearly the busybody of the bunch.

"Precisely," Luther frowned. "Now if you'll excuse me." Luther jerked the wheels of his chair to get them rolling.

"Wow, who knew there was so many Martin Luthers,"

said Martin as he stepped in front of Luther's wheelchair, blocking his way. "I guess we was destined to be pals, eh, Luther, my boy?" Martin held out his hand warmly. Luther responded by pushing his chair over Martin's foot and scuttling quickly out of the activities room.

"Ow!" Martin nearly squealed.

"Welcome to Blessed Acres," the smart one mumbled under her breath.

• • •

Blessed Acres was a bigger bore than Luther ever imagined it would be. He was mad at his daughter, Marsha, all over again for forcing him to come here. What kind of daughter locks her father up in a home full of loonies and half-wits?

With hard pounds of his pointer finger, Luther dialed Marsha's number. He was using an analog because he refused to have one of those cellular things, out of principle.

"And what principle would that be?" Marsha asked him with the same twang of exasperation her mother used to get.

"My principle!" Luther yelled, closing the matter for good.

"Hello!" he hollered into the phone when the voicemail answered.

"—leave your name and number and I'll get back to you as soon as possible."

"Hello!" Luther hollered again.

The voicemail beeped.

"Dammit!" Luther slammed down the phone, knocking it off the table. He left it there because there was no way for him to reach it from his wheelchair.

⋯

"You need to get out of this chair and start walking Luther," the doctor said as he scribbled some notes on a pad.

"Easier said than done," Luther mumbled.

"Well, I guess that's true," the doctor said. "But your ankle's all healed. And if you don't use it, you'll lose it."

"It's already lost," Luther sneered.

"I'm ordering physical therapy three times a week," the doctor continued. "You have to at least try, Luther."

Try. It's what his daughter kept telling him.

"Try to meet people. Try to go outside. Try the activities. Try! Try! Try!" Was there any more patronizing word in the whole English language?

"Oh, I almost forgot," Luther remembered as he was about to leave. "I need a medication change."

"What for?" the doctor's brow crinkled.

"The stuff you have me on is giving me nightmares."

"What kind of nightmares?" the doctor drew out his pen again.

"What do you mean, *what kind of nightmares*?"

"I mean, what happens in them?"

"Well," Luther began reluctantly. "There's these two giant chickens chasing me. One's got two, enormous beach balls tied to its chest, and the other that won't stop making this horrible cackling voice." He shuddered at the memory of it.

"That's not the medication," the doctor shook his head as he scribbled on his pad once more. "I'm writing you another order. I want you to see the counselor."

"Counselor?!" Luther looked as if he'd been shot in the face.

"Yes," the doctor said sternly. "And I'm putting you on an antidepressant."

"I'm not depressed!" Luther nearly shouted.

"Tell it to the counselor," the doctor ended the appointment.

• • •

Marsha finally came for a visit a few days later. Luther did his best to ignore her.

"Come on, dad," she said in that same exasperated tone. "You can't ignore me forever."

"Why are you here?" Luther eventually said.

"To visit you," Marsha collapsed into an armchair.

"What do you want?"

"I don't want anything."

"Bull," Luther spat. "You always wanted something. That's the only reason you ever did come around."

The words stung hard. "Not anymore," Marsha said sadly. "It hasn't been that way for 12 years, and you know it."

"People don't change," Luther waved his hand dismissively.

"What do you want me to say," Marsha stood up and threw her hands in the air. "You want me to say what I've said a thousand times: I'm sorry. I know I was a drug addict and a user, and I took and took from you and mom for years and years. But that all stopped 12 years ago. Mom saw it in her heart to forgive me. Why can't you?"

"Because you put me in this place!" Luther yelled as he turned to face her.

"What choice did we have?" Marsha nearly pleaded. "You crashed the car. You feel down the stairs and broke your ankle. You can't even walk." By now she was in tears.

"Why can't I live with you?"

"Dad, you know that's not possible. I work all day. I take care of the kids at night. There would be no one to take care of you."

"I can take care of my own damn self."

"You almost burned the house down!"

There was a long silence.

"I have to go," she bent down to kiss him, but he turned away. "I'll call you sometime next week." She furiously wiped away tears as she closed the door.

• • •

A few days later, there was a knock at Luther's door.

"Go away!" Luther called.

The knocking continued. He wheeled to the door and flung it open, causing the two ladies to stumble back.

"I said, go away!" he tried to shut the door but the smart lady held it open.

"You nearly bowled us over," she glared. The short, busty one stood next to her, beaming as she held out a plate full of cookies.

"What's that?" Luther grimaced.

"What does it look like," the smart one shot back.

The short lady set the plate on his lap, after which an uncomfortable silence followed.

"Are you going to invite us in?" smiled the short lady.

"No," Luther grunted as he closed the door hard.

"I told you this was a waste of time," the tall lady's muffled voice said behind the door.

Luther pushed himself to the kitchen where he dumped the cookies into the trash can.

• • •

"Is this really necessary?" Luther said as the physical therapist, who called himself Ned, folded Luther's right leg and then his left.

"Yes," Ned answered. "Gets the muscles moving and the blood flowing. Now, I want you to fold them on your own. First one, and then the other."

Luther reached out with both hands to clutch at his right leg.

"No," Ned blocked his hands. "Without your hands." Luther wrinkled his nose in annoyance. He moved his right leg up slightly and was surprised by the sudden burst of pain, making a small grunt.

"The longer you hold back from using them, the worse that pain is going to get," Ned said. "Now the left one."

Luther grimaced as he lifted his left leg. The pain was even worse.

"Good," Ned smiled. "I want you to do that five times with each leg in the morning and in the evening. Gotta get your muscles back in shape."

"Five times," Luther said loudly. "Are you joking?"

"No, I'm not." At that moment, Ned the physical therapist struck Luther as a man who did not joke.

"It going to take a while to get you up and running," Ned continued. "But we'll get you there. Step by step."

• • •

"You're wasting your time," Luther said quietly. "I don't want to talk."

"That's fine," smiled the counselor who had introduced herself as Joan. "We don't have to talk. We can just sit here together." She folded her hands and sat back in her chair looking at nothing in particular.

There was a long, awkward pause.

"This is stupid," Luther finally said.

"Well, what would make it better?" Joan said.

"Oh no," Luther shook his head. "You're not going to get me to talk that way."

"Okay," she said.

"Where do you people get off anyway," Luther sneered.

"I'm not sure what you mean by that."

"Asking dumb questions, giving more medicine, making people talk, forcing them to walk. This ain't no old folks home. It's a loony bin!" Luther finished with real anger.

"You don't like it here, do you, Luther," Joan said with genuine concern.

"Damn right I don't," Luther fumed. "What's there to like? The food is atrocious. The residents are imbeciles. The staff is even worse."

"I think the staff are pretty nice myself," Joan laughed. Luther stopped, suddenly feeling that he was being unfair.

"I just," he started before pausing. "It was never supposed to be this way."

"What do you mean?"

"We were supposed to be together forever. We were supposed to leave together. I wasn't supposed to be left behind."

"Life often does not turn out the way we want it to, Luther," Joan said in a caring tone. "It's okay to be upset, even angry. Especially when we lose someone or we end up in a place we didn't necessarily want to be. But in the end, when things turn out different than the way we imagined, all we can do is make the best of it. Life is much too short to hold on to resentments."

Luther could only nod.

• • •

Later that day, Luther wheeled himself out to the back garden. It actually felt good to breathe in the fresh air and to be in the sunshine. He found a bit of shade and settled in with a book, *War and Peace*. He'd been meaning to read it for as long as he could remember. A chapter or so in, he was dozing in the warmth of the day when he was awakened by an intense squeaking sound.

Luther shifted his chair toward the sound. It was coming from a stand of bushes along the garden path. There was some slight movement near the roots of one of the bushes. Luther focused on the spot and saw the distinctive flutter of a wing. He tried to bend lower to see what kind of bird it was. Out of a gap in the bushes stared two bright, yellow eyes. Luther jumped back sending the creature shuffling across the grass.

It was a small owl, and it was dragging one of its wings. It turned back to look at Luther before disappearing into a nearby stand of trees. Luther pulled something from his pocket, a packet of beef jerky. It was his favorite snack, and he had to hide it from the staff.

"It makes you constipated," the doctor insisted.

Luther ripped a piece and tossed it toward the trees. The owl popped out of the darkness, nabbed the bit of meat, and swallowed it whole. It turned to face Luther, its head leaning sideways as if to measure him.

"You want some more?" Luther showed the owl the bag. He picked out another piece and lobbed it to the owl who caught it in midair.

"There you go," Luther said. "Lot's more here. You just have to come and get it." He waved the bag, and the owl answered with a screech. Luther took the rest of the jerky and spread it out on his lap. The owl watched him intently.

"Come over here, and it's all yours," he said. The owl stepped back into the shadow of the trees. Luther could make out its eyes in the darkness. He knew getting the owl on his lap was a long shot. He started to put the pieces of jerky back in the bag when he heard a piercing screech. Out of the trees the owl bounded straight onto Luther's lap to gobble up the meaty bits.

It was the chance Luther had been waiting for. He threw his blanket over the owl and gently wrapped it up. It screeched for a moment, then went limp. Quickly, he took it back to his room and set it on the bathroom floor where he let it eat its fill of jerky.

• • •

Luther was a veterinarian for over forty years before he retired. He specialized in difficult surgeries for cats and dogs, but he worked with a good many birds in his time as well. The owl clearly had a broken wing. It needed to be set and tended to, or the owl would not survive.

Luther knew if he told the staff, they would call someone to take the owl away, but Luther wanted to be the one to take care of it. He couldn't tell Marsha, because she would just tell the staff. Because he was in a wheelchair, he could not take care of the owl himself. There was only one alternative.

Luther gnashed his teeth as he wheeled into the commissary.

"Look what the cat dragged in," said the tall lady with a smirk.

"Luther, my boy!" Martin greeted warmly. "We was just talking about you."

"Oh?" Luther was immediately suspicious.

"We was talking about famous Luthers," Martin grinned. "Turns out there's a lot!"

Luther made a harumph sound.

"Hilda there," Martin pointed at the busty lady. "She came up with Luther Vandross."

"I like the way he sings," Hilda winked. Then she sang: "You are my star, my guiding light, my fantasy".

"And Minnie," Martin motioned to the tall one. "She mentioned—"

"Lex Luthor," Minnie interrupted. "You know, the bad guy in Superman. You kind of remind me of him," she said directly at Luther.

"I haven't come up with one yet," Martin said.

Luther wanted so badly to tell them how undignified it was to have one's name turned into a game. But if he did that, he would have no one to help him with the owl.

"Luther Burbank," he said through gritted teeth.

"Who?" Martin responded.

"Luther Burbank," Luther repeated. "He was a botanist."

"Oh yes!" Minnie brightened. "Creator of the Russet Burbank potato, among other things. Now why didn't I think of that."

"Oh, I love potatoes," Hilda gushed. "I can eat them any old way. Baked, fried, mashed, boiled."

"It's a very versatile vegetable." Martin added, beaming at his own observation.

"A potato is not a vegetable," Luther halted the conversation.

"What is it then?" said an abashed Martin.

"Any idiot can tell the truth between a root and a vegetable," Luther growled.

"There's nothing to say that a root is not a kind of vegetable," Minnie said while giving Luther a hard look. "A lot of things are mistaken for vegetables anyway, like tomatoes and avocados."

"Tomatoes and avocados aren't vegetables?" Hilda said with a confused look.

"No dear," Minnie said gently. "They're both considered fruits."

"Fruits, you say!" Martin laughed.

"I need some help!" Luther nearly shouted, which was followed by all three looking at him with wide eyes. "If you want to help me with something," Luther said nervously. "Please meet me in my room after lunch."

As Luther maneuvered himself out into the hall, the three sat for a long time, not quite knowing what to say.

● ● ●

An hour or so later, there was a knock on Luther's door. He cringed before opening it slowly. Hilda and Minnie were standing there staring at him.

"Well?" Minnie said. "What's this about?"

"Where's the bald fellow?" Luther asked.

"You hurt his feelings when you called him an idiot," Minnie said matter-of-factly.

The air was suddenly filled with an obnoxious screech, causing both ladies to step back.

"What in Heaven's name?" said Minnie.

"Hurry up and come in!" Luther ushered them into his room.

The owl was perched on Luther's bed eyeing both of the ladies. Its left wing was drooping at its side.

"This is why you need help," Hilda said in understanding.

"Yes," Luther said quietly.

"That's easy," Minnie said as she grabbed the doorknob. "Staff will know exactly what to—"

"No, wait!" Luther nearly begged. "They'll just take him away." And a tear ran down his cheek. Suddenly he felt the grief of his lost wife, and lost life, take hold of him, and he could hold it back no more. Both ladies stood watching with wide eyes, not knowing what to say.

"I can fix him," Luther said in a shaky voice. "I'm a veterinarian. All I need is a few things to patch him up."

"And you want our help," Minnie said in a much softer tone than she had used until now.

"What do you need, Luther?" Hilda said.

"A few dozen tongue depressors, some wood glue, and a good ace bandage should do it," he said. "And, of course, he needs food."

"What does he eat?" Hilda asked.

"Raw meat," Luther answered.

"Leave the meat to me," Hilda said with a wink. Minnie took the task of obtaining the medical supplies.

Getting the meat was actually pretty easy. Edgar, the day cook, had an eye for Hilda's ample bosom, often flirting openly with her when she was in the cafeteria line. She could probably get a whole side of beef from him, no problem, but reserved her request to a few pounds of ground round. Edgar was so eager to please, that she didn't even have to make up a story about why she wanted the meat.

"Anything for such a lovely lady," he fawned.

Minnie's task was much more difficult, and doing so made her feel like a bit of a criminal. The wood glue, she took from the art closet. The depressors and bandages, she pilfered from the medical closet in the examination room when she was left waiting to be examined by the doctor. Luther enjoyed this part most of all. Anything to get back at that annoying doctor.

For several months, the owl recovered in his makeshift sling. He bounded about the small apartment, getting into just about everything. He opened cabinets and tossed plastic cups everywhere. He seemed to like the sound of them clanging on the floor. He taught himself how to turn on the faucet where he would happily sit under the running water until Luther turned it off again.

Luther faithfully tended to the wing, making adjustments on the sling several times a day. The ladies delighted in feeding the owl who they had taken to calling Olsen. For his part, Olsen relished the attention, and seemed to understand that these people were his nursemaids.

The three of them took turns watching Olsen in order to make sure that the staff did not find out about him. Hilda would tuck him into her purse when it was time for staff to clean Luther's room. Minnie would dutifully remove any sign of the owl before the cleaning staff arrived. The routine worked well, and the staff never discovered Luther's feathered charge.

Eventually, Olsen shrugged off his sling and flapped his massive wings, causing papers to unsettle on Luther's desk. He no longer hopped, but instead launched himself from room to room. Thanks to Luther, his wing was fully functional.

"It's time to let you go," Luther said sadly a few days later.

So they made arrangements to take Olsen out one evening after dinner. They placed him in Hilda's bag. Luther held the bag in his lap. Minnie wheeled Luther out onto the foyer with Hilda quietly following. All of them were dreading this day.

When they got to the hedge and the stand of trees, Luther opened the bag. Olsen's snow-white face and beady black eyes stared up at him.

"This is it buddy," Luther said.

Luther took Olsen out of the bag and set him on his lap. Olsen sat there for a moment, looking at each of them in turn almost as if to say *thank you*. Then he turned his head toward the trees, and lifted silently into the air. He was gone in less than an instant. They all stayed there for a long time. Until Luther finally spoke.

"Thank you, my friends," he said. "For all your help."

As they headed back into the building discussing plans to meet for breakfast the following morning, Martin walked by in the hallway.

"Hey, Martin," Luther called. Martin stopped but didn't turn around. "What about famous Martins. Like Martin Van Buren."

"The eighth President of the United States," Minnie added encouragingly.

"I like Martin Short," Hilda said. "He's very funny."

"Martin Scorsese is also very talented," Minnie continued.

"Oh, and Martin Sheen, so handsome," Hilda giggled.

"Martin Landau was a great actor," said Minnie.

"Hm," the sound Luther made halted the conversation for a moment. "There sure are a lot more Martins than there are Luthers, aren't there." Martin still didn't turn around or respond. "But I think the best one of all those is still the two Martin Luthers."

"I guess they are," Martin suddenly turned around. And they all went back to Luther's room where the ladies regaled Martin with the story of Olsen. With Martin's help, Luther stood up so that he could slowly walk to the kitchen to pour everyone some pineapple juice.

"My wife always says it's good for the digestion," he insisted as he passed out the cups with a beaming smile.

The Egg

An egg appeared out of nowhere.

It was the biggest egg anyone had ever seen, nearly as big as a car.

Some people thought it might belong to some rare, exotic, unknown species. Other people thought it might be a boulder that happened to be shaped like an egg. Still, others thought it might be a humongous fungus or some kind of weird mushroom.

Scientists were called in to figure out what it was.

A zoologist put his ear against it, and listened for a very long time. A geologist measured it in several places, and tapped it with a small hammer. A botanist scraped off a sample, and peered at it through a microscope.

None of them could figure out what it was.

A kid, who was watching the whole thing on TV, said, "They need to keep it warm." So a farmer surrounded it with a bunch of heaters and wrapped it in quilts that his wife had sown.

There was nothing to do but wait and see.

For years it went on this way until the egg was all but forgotten.

Then, the leaders decided that they could no longer waste the power to heat an empty egg. The following morning, the heaters would be turned off.

But when the farmer showed up bright and early to pull the plug, the egg was gone.

It was never seen again.

The kid grew up into an old man, and he told his great grandkids the story. His great grandkids said, "But what does it mean?" To which he replied, "Sometimes it's best not to know."

About the Author

David Fallon has a Masters in Clinical Psychology and has devoted a good portion of his life to serving the underprivileged, primarily those who are homeless. He has been writing since he was eight years old as a way of expressing thoughts and stories, both fictional and personal. He has published plays, poems, and short stories in various collections, anthologies, and journals. Most recently, DSTL Arts has published many of his short stories in their ***Conchas y Café Zine*** collections. He has also published several non-fiction articles with Sam Quinones' project, ***Tell Your True Tales***, many of which are based on his work with the homeless in Hollywood. His first short story collection, ***Longing for the Moon***, is the culmination of the tumultuous years following the death of his mother. Many of the stories were written as a way of dealing with loss. Many are filled with the joy that can only be found in relationships. At its heart, ***Longing for the Moon*** is the writer searching for meaning in a complex, often nonsensical world. David is currently working on a novel entitled ***Lefty*** as well as a second collection of stories entitled ***Freedom Rings***.

This publication was produced by DSTL Arts.

DSTL Arts is a nonprofit arts mentorship organization that inspires, teaches, and hires emerging artists from underserved communities.

To learn more about DSTL Arts, visit online at:

DSTLArts.org

CPSIA information can be obtained
at www.ICGtesting.com
Printed in the USA
LVHW041521020622
720264LV00001B/60